EVERYONE ON THE MOON
IS ESSENTIAL PERSONNEL

EVERYONE ON THE MOON

STORIES : JULIAN K. JARBOE

IS ESSENTIAL PERSONNEL

LETHE
PRESS

ISBN 978-1-59021-692-7

Cover artwork by Kim Hu // kim-hu.com
Cover and interior layout by Peter Barnfather
Type set in Bergamo Pro, FontSite Inc. // Google Noto Emoji

for Maya

CONTENTS

Realizing that I have nothing left to lose in my actions
I let my hands become weapons, my teeth become weapons,
every bone and muscle and fiber and ounce of blood become
weapons, and I feel prepared for the rest of my life.

— David Wojnarowicz
Close to the Knives: A Memoir of Disintegration

THE MARKS OF AEGIS

The first nice thing I ever did to my body was tear it open.

Before then, my standard cruelty to myself was taking things in that hurt and holding them there. I said yes when I meant no: at work, at dinner, in parked cars. I tried to annihilate myself through abundance, absorbing and sloshing and wallowing along. I wanted to be swollen with misery.

When I couldn't make enough of my own troubles I took on other people's. I swallowed or inserted or injected some friend's wretched situation and the accessories of their wretchedness, and in there they stayed, building up in the junkyard of abuse under my smooth young skin. God, I had great skin.

It got to be that one day I was tired. I could not tell want from habit. There weren't friends left to take on troubles from, and the work was done, the plate empty, the cars driven home and tucked away in roomy garages beneath sleeping families.

Well, I'm practical when I'm nothing else. I got out my box cutter and I started making ways out. I sliced along the planes of my skin and squeezed until everything on the inside that ought not to have been there was on the outside again. I expected to recognize each individual trouble, but everything had melded together into a civilization of its own.

I cleaned it up with my best detergents, slowly and methodically. A whole city emerged. All the people I had used had formed alliances with one another, built striking homes from the rough materials I'd left them with. Their culture may have started in filth but it had changed and grown. Their buildings floated and spun in slow orbit of one another. Every wall was a doorway and every stair a hall and every window a skylight or escape hatch depending on the rotation of the structure at given moment.

I called it Aegis and admired it, and thought about maybe putting it back inside me to keep forever. It was a really beautiful place with so many inhabitants who deserved that beauty. I thought I deserved a little beauty, too. But when it started to float higher and away I saw that it didn't need me anymore, and I decided to end our association on more gentle terms that it had begun. I opened the window and sent it on its away, crying as it swept into the breeze. Aegis is still out there, thriving I think.

Then it was done, so I closed myself back up. When I ran through the first aid kit I used the sewing kit and when I ran through that I used the soldering iron. Then I took a very long, very hot shower.

Some people see my stitched and bandaged gashes and my cauterized holes and say, there goes a bitch who has really fucked herself up for good. There goes a real mess. They think they've seen a tragedy. But these people don't know the first thing about scars. They'll never understand how I could be so proud.

HERE YOU ARE, NEAR ME

Parvaneh walked to the coffee shop in her cleanest shirt and dress slacks at rush hour, just to hold onto ritual and routine, now that she no longer had a job to structure her weekday. All it took was one ultra-popular friend retweeting her grouchy hot take on the manager with the simmering bigotries—not even naming names—to launch her from being a person with a job and a Twitter account to being a martyr in the fight against office microaggressions. A clickbait mill retweeted the retweet, quoted and linked it at the top of their big feature about harassment, which had the effect of funneling all new harassment into her mentions and, soon enough, her personal email, her work email, and the work email of her human resources director, whose fifteen minute review of the situation left her circling the cream and sugar island in the The Bee's Buzz instead of having anywhere else to be on a Monday morning.

She took the entire shaker of chocolate powder with her to a round table in the back of the cafe and tapped on the three-hundred unread messages alert on her phone.

Strangers were indignant about her original gripe. They called her a liar, a slut, a terrorist, variations thereof, and threatened to perform all manner of violences on her. One by one, she screenshot, blocked, and reported the messages, as if this might do some minor good like tossing back a single dried-out starfish into a polluted sea. Doing this without letting herself read them was a lesser of two anxiety attacks. But this morning, as abruptly as she'd become unemployed, the vitriol dwindled, and the pictures started.

The first picture came with a note: "I saw your story and your avatar and the documents about you and I recognized you from this photo that hangs in our first floor hallway. See attached."

The attachment was a photo of that aforementioned photo, in its frame, in the wallpapered hallway. A white family—mom, dad, goth-looking daughter, startled-looking son—smooshed together in front of the Byrd Weatherbee statue in the University neighborhood where The Bee's Buzz operated as well. All of their hands touched Byrd's brass foot, a tourist-folk tradition for good luck which persisted in spite of the Weatherbee University hazing standard to piss on that same foot late at night, after their proud parents have stumbled drunk into rideshares and been whisked away like reverse-Cinderellas to luxury hotels.

In the background of this photo, Parvaneh saw herself sitting by the statue, shoving a bagel in her face, with wet hair, adding an unintended layer of sloppy reality to an otherwise idyllic family portrait. She looked up from her phone and her drink and out the front window of the coffee shop, where she could glimpse the left elbow of Weatherbee's brass akimbo stance behind a swarm of pedestrians.

Parvaneh squirmed. How many photographs existed of her in the albums of strangers? This partial answer was tantalizing. More of them arrived throughout her first week of unemployment, from different kinds of people, in all corners of the city. There were more families, couples, packs of friends, selfies, the creative commons licensed photo from the Wikipedia page about the Byrd Weatherbee statue. In every single one, she was present, walking, sitting, eating her lunch, picking her nose, rifling through her purse, finishing a beer, reading a book. Sometimes, just waiting for something, a train or last call or the laundromat dryer. In several, she looked right into the camera with the beginning of motion in her stance, her gaze already drifting unaware to the next blip of interaction with the lives of others. The torrent of threats evaporated, but neither were these new messages friendly in any conventional sense. Each one said some variation of the same simple description: "here you are, near me."

SELF CARE

Fuckos in this stupid town think nobody notices how when the tide just keeps coming in without going out again that "some" neighborhoods get sunk forever as an "unfortunate side effect of coastal flooding" while others become the sexy hip cool new "seafloor village." I'd cackle every time some bullshit golden-brick seawall crumbles and takes another mansion with it, but now there's straight-up UNDERWATER house tours for a zillion dollars a ticket, the same way they used to show off their giant Christmas trees and shit but even more pretentious cause now I guess they host in designer scuba gear. "Oh, this old thing? Blub blub, there's sand in my butt, no wait it's diamonds, ha ha!" (That's how they talk probably.) MEANWHILE where MY shitty old apartment used to be is now an undersea God-damned HOTEL AND CASINO. In a cute little dome bubble park and everything!!! Like imagine if when the Titanic sunk they were just like "fuck it, we'll make it work if we can disappear the poor people corpses, we've GOT to make back our investment SOMEHOW" and everyone was like "oh my God of course that's so important!" So I got to know some of my favorite sidewalks for a bit, and wouldn't you know it, "extreme weather" means something else entirely when you LIVE OUTSIDE!

Like yeah it gets cold and hot at the "wrong" times if you're some kind of child prince whose gonna cry to daddy if you don't get snow when you go skiing and sunshine when you step foot on your yacht (HA HA HA bite me). You want wind in your sails, fucko? I can tell you ALL about the wind! I had sex with this guy in a parking lot one night and something broke the sound barrier right as he climaxed and it was just as likely some freak Climate Event off the fucked up ocean as it might have been a super-sonic cum-fart (it was so cute though, he was like "what" and "are you okay?" which was sweet of him and we didn't exchange names or anything too personal but honestly it's good to know there are still some GENTLEMEN around here). It's summer and it's freezing and sometimes the clouds pick up debris or something falls from a drone or a plane or whatEVER is happening up there and there are heavy metal balls of sleet or oily raindrops that catch fire as they fall. Bon voyage!

I had a PREMIUM spot near that parking lot, too, and everything was FINE until clearly someone snitched and an autoplow swept on by and took ALL MY STUFF AWAY atop a rolling conglomerate of rubble like a garbage fairy's trash sleigh off to deliver bad luck to all the world's ugly children. My cover was blown and I could only sleep in the stock room at Fatima's Psychic Emporium And Tee Shirts between clopening shifts, so yes, I did EVENTUALLY have to stay in a church for a while but I AM STILL A WITCH.

Our Lady of Good Voyage had a stupid mandatory intake process with this whiny-ass support group. The facilitator's name was either Apollo or Olive Garden. We went around and did our little introductions but it escalated into feel-good therapy shit faster than any street hustle and I wanted nothing more than to get kicked in the teeth listening to it. Everyone talked like they'd invented feelings. This one person was so hung up on not suffering enough to feel like they could REALLY call themselves marginalized and Apollo or Olive Garden was all "blah blah I affirm that your identity is valid" and I said, "EXCUSE ME but if anyone would like to make ME feel valid I will be passing around this fully-compostable coffee cup I found for direct donations!" Apollo or Olive Garden told me to "step back" (i.e. SHUT UP) so I called them all tourists and kicked over my folding chair and TRIED to escape.

I was making to leave like, "fuck it, fuck this, fuck you, I'm flinging myself into the sea, she can fucking have me," and they took it SO SERIOUSLY that this priest got involved blockading the exit and asking if he could "help" me in that way store security always ask if they can "help" you when they think you're gonna steal something. The facilitator was all, "where do you think you're going?" and I shouted, "TO GET KICKED IN THE TEETH. WHY NOT? IT'S FREE AND IT BEATS JOINING THIS COMA COLLECTIVE!" So the priest made me go to his office with him and I was like, "WHAT, ARE YOU GOING TO GIVE ME DETENTION? DOES THIS GO ON MY PERMANENT RECORD, FATHER?"

He just smiled like a little lap dog and said he'd been "called by God to serve where the need was greatest," and I said, "That's what I've been TRYING TO SAY: I HAVE A LOT OF NEEDS."

He LAUGHED. "Yes, I can see that!" He was short and swarthy and sort of hot? Dude had very hip, canary yellow glasses and these eyebrows for days and WAY too tidy a beard for an ostensibly celibate heterosexual. His office door said FR. GASPREN in an extremely serious font and inside there was a human skull on his desk (which really took me back) and a television with a wrestling match on mute and a framed print of the praying hands emoji on the wall, and that's when I was like, ohhhh, he's a Cool, Accessible Priest. Okay, SURE.

We had a little chit chat about my situations and he had the sheer audacity to say, "That sounds awful." It was that practiced, calm, do-gooder, care-worker voice I hate. Fake as hell. If you want to witness my anger then GET ANGRY ALONGSIDE ME!!!

Father Gaspren kept asking me things like "What does community mean to you, Anthony?" and I said, "Isn't that YOUR job?" I knew about group solipsism and infighting and cults and love quadrangles and underground scenes and mutually assured annihilation but I did not know this "community" queen. Never heard of her!

"Now, more than ever, is the time to join our community of mercy and compassion through Christ," he said. "You don't have to lie to Him or to me. There's no gatekeeping here, no shareholders, and no research study. No academic thesis. You get help no matter what."

I called BULLSHIT. It was not exactly my first time dealing with priests. I look like the exact type of person who gets excommunicated, and I enumerated my MANY good reasons to be suspicious and how I ran away from Sunday School and became a gay transsexual WITCH.

"Well, we don't refuse any type of person," he said. Then he slipped right into the scam: I could stay in the on-site dormitory for "free" in exchange for a bunch of chores and also I had to come to Mass on Sundays but there were donuts and coffee. I asked him if the donuts and coffee were also free and he gave me this satisfied nod and I realized that by asking a follow-up question, I'd admitted defeat. God had me in xer clammy hands once again like some huge cosmic joke but I was also impressed by the power move of the whole thing, which only goes to prove I am the pervert they always said I was.

But there is ALWAYS a catch.

"However," he added, and I gave him every non-verbal way I have of saying: called it! "If you expect relaxed attitudes about sexual ethics, I'm afraid you'll be disappointed. There will be no 'cruising' or 'turning tricks' or 'back alley' activities tolerated." He gave me that swollen look like he wanted to do some random acts of kindness at me which is a thousand times worse than any rival witch's evil eye. The REAL creeps in this world are optimists.

He took me to the dormitories and I guess it made sense to have us do chores because nobody there was about to fill the coffers. The group bathrooms and makeshift kitchenette with all the knives and matches in a locked pantry and the sweaty asbestos musk of old linoleum floors meant I just KNEW without asking that I was going to be told when to eat and sleep.

The bedrooms were gender segregated but FOR SOME REASON I ended up sharing with the only other transsexual even though we were going different directions (the reason was transphobia). She was this tall beautiful butch with stone gray eyes named "Bert, short for Roberta," which she said in one breath with no inflection. She told me that she was a trucker even though there are only ex-truckers. I said I was a witch and she snorted and asked, "what, like with the pointy hats?" and I said "yes" even though I do not physically own any kind of hat because it was still emotionally true.

The Church always gets its cassocks in a twist about witches but witchcraft has all the props I do like about religion that I first acquired in church anyway:

1. singing and chanting in dead languages,
2. lighting things on fire,
3. impractical headgear.

"Ain't spiritual, ain't agnostic, ain't open minded," Bert said. "Don't wanna hear about no gods or masters or mystical woo-woo. Ask me my sign and I'll never talk to you again."

"Oh, I would never ask," I said. "I know how Scorpios need their privacy."

For an ETERNITY that passed in the next minute I thought that she might kill me, but then she spat out this big laugh and said, "Oh, it's on, witch," and she said "witch" exactly like she meant "bitch" so I decided that I liked her. I traded her a Percocet for cigarettes and that sealed the deal. Trans solidarity is fucking BEAUTIFUL.

We went outside to smoke. Everything on the grounds was crammed together on a slip of a sandbar with the dormitory and a shed back toward mainland and this menacing black lighthouse called The Sin Seer at the far rocky precipice over the sea. One more big hurricane and the whole place was obviously going down like frown. The church itself even looked like an overturned ship with this massive wooden arch and stained glass porthole windows. Once upon a time people made boats AND buildings this close to the water out of wood which seems insane because I'm pretty sure wood melts???

Bert and I sucked through half a pack and watched the waves flop on the thin, clumpy, petrified "beach" until that flaccid support group got out and dispersed like an infection. Apollo or Olive Garden looked at me and started to come over. They waved and smiled, in the way of sick confused little children who run back towards conflict because it gives them meaning, and I thought, what the hell: life is short, treasure moments of radical vulnerability and speaking my truth, so I tossed down my cigarette and flipped them off with BOTH of my hands.

Bert and I got to talking some more. We had very different kinds of terrible lives and not really too much in common but she NEVER once called me valid, THANK GOD, and that's why we were best friends.

I didn't like to spend a lot of my days off work at Fatima's hanging around Our Lady of Good Voyage because it bummed me the fuck out. There was a huge dark painting of Mary in the chapel. Everything about the picture was severe. The clouds looked like packing foam and the folds of her blue cloak were rigid as a bendy straw. It made me miss my mom and feel bad about my abortions.

Father Gaspren said all that stuff about a totally accepting and welcoming community but he still had all these posters outside his office about "forgiveness" for all the shit people do to their own selves. One HUGE purple one with a crying lady on it gave a number and a website for a "Christ-Is Pregnancy Center" and you know what it even advertised "grief counseling for men" but SOMEHOW I KNEW that they didn't mean me, a man who terminated a fetus or two in my day and maybe HYPOTHETICALLY could be interested in counseling from all the GRIEF everybody gave me about it! Like if people NEED TO BE FORGIVEN for their own private business then they aren't really being taken exactly as they are SO WHICH ONE WAS IT?

I was at Sunday Mass feeling sorry for myself and not allowed to nibble the bread or sip the wine and NERVOUS because that week Father Gaspren found and confiscated my drugs and I was staring at the Sad Mom Painting and the horde of sweaty parishioners praised and prayed along when Father Gaspren announced the end of a partnership between the local diocese and a tenant's rights group because of their "lack of support for the unborn."

"There is a tragic sense of lost opportunity," he said. There sure was! Even the free donuts and coffee would not fill up the bottomless pit of lost opportunities going down in Our Lady of Good Voyage.

Bert looked plain bored. I whispered to her, "Let's go literally anywhere else that isn't here," and she nodded, arms crossed like the opposite of crucifixion, and we strode out from the room not even pretending we had to pee or anything. I told her, "I have a new activity plan. Let's hex the gentry."

Bert shook her head. "Won't dignify that mumbo jumbo."

I explained that a good hex requires objects that have had a lot of direct contact with the intended victim, which meant helping me gather supplies also meant I'd show her some especially good residential trash picking spots. THAT at least was secular enough for her, plus she got an unopened pair of socks out of it. Meanwhile I got all the sneaky little personal items I could find, and we took the spoiled spoils back to the eroded beach outside Our Lady and I drew a ring in the crappy sand and placed the junk within it.

"Circle of rubble; refuse of gentries," I chanted. "Now I set my intention."

Bert frowned harder than normal.

"A curse on every opulent flip, eviction renovation, up-and-coming investors-take-notice neighborhood renewal, be it by land, sea, or sky. May the benefactors, be they knowing or unknowing, have bathroom doors that open the wrong way and get banged up on the sink."

"Heh."

"May their desalinators break in the middle of a feast day. May they forget their passcodes and microwave their dermal chips and replacement is a lengthy and costly process. May their virtual assistants transcribe them wrong in all sensitive matters and sext their bosses. May they discover as each light breaks—no wait, I have a better one than that: may all their sentient vacuums and talking dishwashers and robot nannies malfunction and need parts that are no longer in production."

"Leave the robots alone," Bert muttered.

"What should it matter who I curse? I thought you didn't believe in any of it anyway."

"Leave them alone even in your delusions."

"Bert, you used to be a trucker!"

"Still a trucker."

"Well you'd still be driving A TRUCK if you hadn't been replaced with a machine."

Bert sat down on the rocks.

"Machine didn't take my rig. They don't take nothing from nobody. They do what they're set in motion to do."

"See, that's what I'm saying. The just-following-orders thing is why everything is so terrible. Everyone cries automaton."

"Thought about getting a few augments myself, just little cyborg stuff like new driving ankles, but I never had the money."

"Yeah, but that's different."

"How's it?"

"Cause THAT'S extremely cool."

"I worked sixteen-hour days every day, and robots can do twenty-four straight. Nothing wrong with that. No self-driving semi ever called me a he-she or pulled a knife out to 'show me' at a rest stop. My navigator was good at getting us where we needed to go and had a no-bullshit attitude built right into her. Nah, I like computers."

She kicked at the garbage circle.

"It was a person who had me finance the thing myself just to get the gig," she added. "And it was a person that seized it right along with all I'd paid when I couldn't afford a repair. It don't matter if they replaced me with a living spaceship or a fleet of oxen. A person set it up that way and a person followed through so it was people that did that to me."

"Bert, you should be, like, an organizer."

"Oh, there's a mass movement, all right. Industry is banding together to make it illegal for anyone more'n half machine to do their crap jobs so they can have their crap jobs back exactly the way they were."

"Hm." It all made sense now. "You have hatched us a much better scheme then curses. The intention of this spell needs to be more potent."

"I did not say that."

I snuck over to the church offices and stole the entire Christ-Is Pregnancy Hotline poster and brochure box and ran them back to the circle before anyone had time to notice. I rolled some up like proper witchy herb bundles and Bert was pissed but then once she read what they were she held out her lighter. We lit them all for ceremony and then we added little sticks and drift junk until we had a proper bonfire going. It started to drizzle grease but every drop that fell near us poofed right up. While an INDIVIDUAL witch such as myself does not have the power to halt or reverse the world's ills, we did do that one TOGETHER, so it was a VERY powerful spell.

When Father Gaspren found out he gave us indefinite bathroom duty and took away my phone for messing with "the occult" and "destruction of church property" so while we had to scrub poop smears and piss puddles, it was worth it.

On our first Doody Duty I asked Bert if I could have the bleach and she said, "I don't know, bitch, can you?" but her eyes were in a way like when she looked at pizza that she got to eat by herself.

"I think I can, bitch, so hand it to me," I said.

"In a minute, bitch, I'm finishing this seat."

"Okay then, bitch, I'll wait!"

It went on that way for a while and that night I had a prophetic dream (one of my strongest powers) that everyone's true name was what they were known for plus "bitch." Bert was Hard Driving Bitch and Father Gaspren was Priest Bitch or Daddy Bitch and so on. The only person without a true name was me. I didn't know what kind of bitch I was. I woke up in a cold sweat and lay awake the rest of the night still smelling like bleach.

The underwater resort fuckos had the nerve to recruit us. Three of them came to Our Lady of Good Voyage in the middle of an afternoon while we were having movie night in the chapel (even though it was daytime we called it movie night; by actual night we had curfew; it was an old dystopian movie about a plucky band of sexy and oppressed teenagers using computer hacking and crossbows to overthrow an evil vice president who murdered the milquetoast devil-you-know president and started a global resource war over fresh water aquifers buried beneath the south pole; the sexy teens temporarily ally with cybernetically-enhanced penguins to defeat their common enemy; we all cheered for the heroes on the screen no matter how little any of us could muster the will to be the clean dishes we wanted to see in the world).

The fuckos brought their various propagandas about how their sub-marine pleasure palace or whatEVER needed more Service And Hospitality Associates and no contribution would go unpunished or some shit. They must have known we would be a variety pack of undesirables because they were the most diverse model minority trio of fuckos. One had an expensive salon version of a do-it-yourself haircut and tattoos on her face. She looked like she'd really turned her shit around with rehab or Jesus or lifestyle blogging. Another wore a truly outstanding impractical religious head thing with some elegant corporate couture. She gave me that icy vibe like she was ready to throw someone under the bus to get promoted, but like a literal bus. The main fucko burst into his pitch right over the best scene in the movie, in this sing-song lisp that is exactly like MY sing-song lisp except I also have a trashy shore town accent on top of it because I happen to be ACTUALLY FROM HERE unlike that TOURIST.

Father Gaspren told them, "Please, no soliciting" and they took it for a joke (I'll give them that one because "Don't come here to forcefully sell things" is kind of a hard line to defend when you're the colonial proselytizer, oopsie doopsie). They tore on about how the ocean was totally habitable now. They'd take anyone who showed up at the marina in time for the morning ferry to the sea elevator. Everything you could need was there and there was plenty of work to do and also whales had once been land animals and had gone back to the water, so why not us?

The thing is, that shit was seductive. All of us listened. Gay Voice McFuckoman made conspicuous eye contact with Bert and she took one of the brochures so I stared him down and hoped he could hear me telepathing that he looked like a red puffy baked potato in a button-down. He glanced at me and I heard him thinking, "I might be gay but at least I'm not a fag like you," and I thought right back, "You're right, we are NOT the same, because you are EMPTY inside while I CARE about these people so at least I'm a CAREFAG while you're just an ELITIST FAGGORATI PRICK!!!"

"You folks really should take your materials and get going," Father Gaspren insisted. The fuckos laughed again. SO RUDE.

"Pardon us, Father," they said. "I thought all were welcome in God's house?"

So I grabbed a thurible and swung it around my head like a slingshot and got in all their faces and chased them out the front steps screaming, "YOU LEAVE GOD'S HOUSE ALONE!" but by the time I came back the movie was completely over. I HATE professionalism and professionals!!!

There was a storm moving in and the rain broke right before we got to our chores so I mostly stabbed at the dirt while water that smelled like shoe polish dribbled through the ceiling and onto the floors I'd just done. I could hear wind whistle through the seams of the building and the spooky little throats of the organ pipes. Nobody talked to each other and Father Gaspren sort of crept from room to room. Shit was over the top drama well before the hurricane sirens or klaxons or whatever started wailing all through town, but for once I was just not worried? Like this one time ever in my life I think I was something approaching comfortable. At bedtime I had this idea to tell Bert about how we might fix the drainage and better hold off the worst of the storm, but right before lights out she told me all flat and factual, "Be taking those people up on the gig."

"It's got to suck. It's probably piecework by the half pennies."

"Probably."

"They don't actually want to give you a job, you know. They want to get rid of you with a one-way ticket out of the way. I bet the chapel is gonna be a luxury condo. They took our homes and now they're trying to buy us out of our right to stay here."

Bert exhaled long and slow through her nose.

"Well, I ain't from here, and where I'm from don't exist anymore. Bottom of the sea'll be about as nowhere as any place else."

I wanted to say something about how this place wasn't NOWHERE with all of us in it but she'd have told me to quit being corny and she'd have been right. Her attention bore into me like a piston and I didn't want to lose it saying something dumb which for me would be saying anything at all and I still thought she might kill me at any moment for any reason and I think that's why I was a LITTLE bit in love with her.

The next morning I woke up to all hell bursting against my one tiny window in my EMPTY room. I started walking around the place and it wasn't just my room, either. They were ALL empty. When I started kind of yelling a bit maybe, Faster Gaspren came out from his twee little suite and confirmed that EVERYONE ELSE was gone to the bottom of the ocean with the fuckos, just like that! We were completely alone in the whole world, like, OH. OKAY.

Fucking SELLOUTS.

Guess those bitches will never have to worry about hurricanes or floods or ME ever again on the COMPLETE OPPOSITE SIDE OF THE WAVES. I flipped off the empty beds then opened the window and leaned out into storm and flipped off the whole town and the clouds, too.

"We should get going to some higher ground," Father Gaspren said. "I don't think Our Lady of Good Voyage is going to make it through without her people." And he said it with this truly sad little voice like he was momentarily a regular person. "It reminds me of walking through the house I grew up in after my parents had died. Of course, that house is gone now, too. The whole Dead Horse Beach village is gone."

I SCREAMED. Like, literally, "Ahhhhh!!!" and "Oh my God!!!" and "I'm from Dead Horse Beach too!!!" I was all, "Hey there, boy next door!!!" and we dished some REAL ancient gossip, I'm talking DEEP neighborhood lore, and made fun of how the developers called the area The Benthic Innovation Quarter now like it wasn't tenements for a zillion years.

"This area has always had problems," he said. "Some of the buildings on that block were abandoned for a long time."

"Yeah! Those were the ones with the best parties."

"Well, they gave a hard face to those problems, and who would not want to make that go away? But to let it all sink, just like that... A world of terror has at its core the god of money and not the people." Back in Priest Mode.

"You would have made a cool punk," I told him.

"Thank you, Anthony."

"But you know what, all the punks I know right now are trying to keep their tenant's rights project from falling to shit. It's too bad there are no entrenched cultural institutions for them to partner with."

"Now, be fair."

"It's just a pity, that's all! The people who should be at the heart of the world or whatever, I guess, are going to lose."

He put a hand on my shoulder. I wondered if he'd ever kissed another man. I thought maybe I should find out.

"Christ and I are here for you, Anthony. We can fight the evil in this world together, through Him."

That was a cheap shot because it would be true if I repressed EVERYTHING ELSE THAT I AM for people (not Jesus though because Jesus would LOVE me and we'd BALL).

From the dorm with the open window we could see and hear the tide crash over the rocks and cliffs and the water pulling closer to The Sin Seer and Our Lady.

"When we get back from waiting this out," I said. "I will clean everything perfectly and fix it all up nice in time for Mass if you'll please, please, please let me take Communion?"

He pulled his hand back to his side.

"That won't be possible, unfortunately."

I obviously was saying "why the fuck not" with my entire face and body cause then he started to back-peddle the whole being-a-person-in-front-of-me thing.

"Perhaps I should not be so candid with you. A change in tone is not a change in doctrine." He stepped away. "We should get going sooner rather than later. I'll meet you in my office in fifteen minutes?"

I said "SURE, FINE" to get him to leave me alone and then instead of packing I gathered my necessary supplies (herbs, balms, chalk, cookies and a juice box), raided the shed for an antique harpoon gun and spears, and barricaded myself inside The Sin Seer's lantern room.

I was the Witch King of Trash Town. The Carefag Bitch That Gave a Fuck. I surveyed my surroundings for enemies. I gathered strength from the elements to better manifest my powers.

"Great uncaring mother of life," I chanted to the ocean. "Drown us all in your watery tiddies. Flood this whole bitch-ass peninsula. Reduce this nightmare to crumbs. Return all our matter to the hungry universe."

The waves covered most of the grounds and pressed against the hatch doors of Our Lady of Good Voyage. After half an hour or so, Father Gaspren hurled one open and trudged out into the storm searching for me. I loaded the harpoon and heaved it onto my shoulders, then leaned over the railings of the lighthouse tower.

"Anthony!" He cried. "We have to leave! Come down!"

"Why don't YOU come up HERE and TRY AND MAKE ME!"

I aimed for his middle. The scrunch in his face shifted from concern to something else. He might not have heard me right, he might have got acid rain in his eyes, or maybe he was considering my challenge at face value and wracked with indecision. The water rose past his knees and kept rising, but he stayed planted where he was and just ogled and yawped like a complete chucklefuck.

"I know how you're feeling!" He shouted, which FIRST of all, how DARE he? "Let's redirect that rage!"

FUCK. NO. EVERYTHING had been taken from me and even the people who tried to help me took away my painkillers and my phone and sometimes my shoelaces. So SECOND of all, I was DONE being "redirected."

I am completely, one-hundred-percent AWARE that if I destroy myself out of spite it's neither confronting nor fixing my problems BUT! You know what? My problems are what I have left to work with! I've even tried heavy-duty therapy and hypnosis and exorcism and all they ever wanted to talk about was my childhood (ZZZZZ BORING) and "relationship patterns" (SNORE). There is ALWAYS A CATCH. Professionals yammer on about the "mental health crisis" in These Turbulent Times, like, GEE I WONDER if it has anything to do with most people being constantly in a state of desperation to sell their joy to oligarchs forever and ever? None of that goes away EVEN IF I could travel back in time and get un-fucked-up.

So I shouted back, "I GET TO KEEP MY RAGE!" I felt it everywhere in everything around me so I knew that I OWNED it and I knew that it was MINE. No more deals, no more feels! No more city, no more pity! My anger is me taking full custody over my body and my space FOR ONCE.

But of COURSE he didn't have a DAMN thing to say to THAT so I added, "SUCK MY FUCK!!!"

Dude had NO idea who he was dealing with. At least I know what kind of BITCH I am.

THE NOTHING SPOTS WHERE
NOBODY WANTS TO STAY

The veil is thin immediately outside the Salmon P. Chase Municipal Junior High School. A dense perimeter of flowering thorns grow two feet out from the exterior walls, and between the plants and the bricks is a zone dense with magical energy. Especially suggestible students and teachers can sense it; the stunted or abused into rupture, the intuitive, those in a state of spiritual drift. Like all liminal spaces, this one can be elusive, and sometimes it's hungry, draws you near and lures you in. It gives, and it takes away.

The school building is newly renovated and the grounds heavily trimmed. It's the drippy-snot-nose part of March in 2002, and the students file outside in assigned pairs because Mike Johnson—

obviously—left a bomb threat on a stall in the yellow wing boy's bathroom, but the teachers are officially telling the students there's a fire drill. They have to be sensitive to the handful of earnestines who take every Sharpie pentagram and locker room firecracker stash at face value. The other four-hundred or so children know that this, like the "rabid dog" lock-downs, is entirely about someone and something else.

Jamie is the only student who has ever experienced the aftermath of public violence, and he wanders away from the crowd with AJ, leaving their assigned buddies to buoy in place with one another. AJ is sure a teacher can see them sneaking off into the bushes, in their ski coats and L.L. Bean super-sized monogrammed reflector tape backpacks, the clacking multitude of novelty key-chains on the zip pull, but nobody stops them. AJ is used to anticipating trouble, even though he's with Jamie, and adults let Jamie do anything he wants now.

Out of view, the boys crouch over the buried treasures of their hiding place, Tupperware and pencil boxes stuffed full of contraband from the strip mall on the edge of town. The underpass and the mall parking garage are both reachable directly through a portal from the junior high school bushes. The portals present themselves when beckoned, but seem to possess a will of their own and something like a sense of humor—once they tried to get to the train station and it deposited them on the tracks with just enough time to dodge the approaching train.

Jamie believes this will is a reflection of his and AJ's subconscious. AJ is not so sure anything that powerful could come from them.

Jamie pops open one of their boxes and pulls out a king-size candy bar they shoplifted last weekend. He twists it in half and they lean against the wall, gnashing at the toffee and the nougat. When they finish, Jamie takes a deep breath, adjusts the crotch of his jeans, and turns to lean onto AJ, pressing his erection against AJ's hips.

"Do you feel that?" he says, and smirks.

"Yeah," AJ responds, and licks the milk chocolate off his hand.

Jamie kisses AJ with tongue, smears of candy still on his lips and stuck in his braces, and rocks his hips on AJ's in a performed and disembodied way, going through the motions with no regard for what might feel good. AJ coughs into the kiss, and Jamie takes it for a moan of pleasure and fishes his hands up under AJ's shirt to fondle his breasts.

AJ's had sizable tits since fifth grade, the only thing about him, he's certain, which earns him some kind of use value for others, an idea so loudly and consistently reinforced by the lust, envy, and scorn of others that his dysphoria around having them at all won't surface consciously for another decade. In 2016, when AJ wakes up from his top surgery, his first thought will be, "well, now I'll have to rely on charm alone."

For now, AJ thinks, they keep Jamie interested, and it mostly feels good. They're achingly heavy, and Jamie grabs them like he's catching a ball, squeezes, pushes them up toward AJ's chin. This is the way every boy will ever touch them, like he can't believe his good luck but needs to relocate them skyward like a button mash code to unlock some next level fondling. It's sloppy, but a welcome relief from gravity, and it's so easy to just stand there and allow it to happen.

AJ wants to touch Jamie in return, kiss Jamie's whole body with his clothes off. For some reason, the thought of acting on these things then and there, in the same semi-public way that Jamie acts on all of his desires, does not occur to AJ.

What does cross his mind is an urge to steal tapes. He passively suggests they head over to the mall for some release.

Jamie's made a wet spot on the crotch of his jeans but tucks himself away and repeats AJ's words as though they are his own.

"Good idea," AJ tells him.

The rest of the school is filing back into the building for the last two and a half class periods of the day, and Jamie wipes his mouth and focuses on opening a portal. He holds AJ's hand because he believes this makes the magic stronger. If a teacher does see them, they're not going to do anything now that Jamie's got that serious look on his face. Jamie doesn't have to take any tests, or even really keep coming to school, and the guidance counselors have recommended private therapists and grief groups but he won't let anybody try to help him, not even his mother, Eileen. Everybody wants Jamie to talk, so they keep telling him yes, and he hates all of them.

AJ doesn't ask Jamie to talk, which is how they've gotten so close, but AJ wants it just as much as everyone else. He thinks that the trick is to be so reliable that any day now, all this time together is going to add up to something meaningful and Jamie will open up, finally, to AJ and nobody else. The saddest boy in the whole school will tell AJ things about his dad, and say "you're the only one who understands," and it will be the single most flattering and fulfilling burden of AJ's whole life. AJ lays in bed at night and imagines the whole scenario. Sometimes he rehearses the hushed, intimate tone he's going to respond in.

They figured out the veil and the portals in the first place because Jamie was looking for a spot to set his diary on fire last Halloween, and AJ had been the one to bring him a lighter and show him how to use it. They burned the barely-filled notebook behind the bushes—what could possibly be in there, AJ wondered, as it burned—and buried the ashes under the mulch, and that's when they saw other transient places in the town, the nothing spots, where nobody lived or worked and nobody wanted to stay for very long, and they could reach out and touch them and step into them and find themselves there.

Jamie tried to use it to go back in time, but it never worked. AJ knew Jamie had tried to go back to September 10th alone, and was never going to ask AJ to go there with him, but he had tried and failed and AJ knew this because one day Jamie got really philosophical about what the portals were and how they worked. People always get deep after they don't get what they really want, AJ thought.

The boys rip a wound in the world and walk through it together, still holding hands. They exit in the food court behind the photo booths, and separate inside Suncoast Video. AJ peels the shrinkwrap off an anime boxset and slips the individual tapes into his cargo pockets while Jamie dumps a handful of coins onto the counter and asks the clerk how much candy he can get for five dollars in loose change. This takes enough time for AJ to inconspicuously slip back out of the store and appear to be idly browsing bachelor party gags in Spencer's Gifts by the time Jamie joins him again. They have it down to routine, but this time Jamie takes more than an hour to rejoin. When he does, AJ is running out of excuses to browse the joke book section without buying anything.

"Sup," Jamie says with forced coolness.

"I don't get what the thing is about mother-in-laws," AJ says, closing a book and returning it to the shelves. "What took so long? Are we in the clear?"

"Yeah, yeah, just had to make a side trip."

They head to the basement level of the mall parking garage and climb through a portal back to school, in time for the procession of SUVs at the front circle. AJ rushes to change out of what he's wearing and back to the clothes he left home in that morning. When he's done, he and Jamie meet out front and climb into the back of Eileen's car for a ride home.

Eileen greets the kids wearing a leather blazer and her hair styled for volume, cinnamon shoulder-length curls. She looks resilient, tired, and handsome. Jamie eyes the luxury jacket with suspicion. He wonders where her cat-hair covered fleece is, her usual abundance of bobby pins coming loose.

"Happy Friday," she sing-songs, and Jamie crosses his arms over his chest. She turns to AJ and asks him if he's attending Crystal Sazerac's sweet thirteen with Jamie that evening.

"Oh yeah," AJ responds, a soft fog of dread setting into his mood. "I'd forgotten about it."

Eileen hums along with the radio as she drives AJ home. The two boys wallow silently, slumped down, AJ with his knees pressed against the seat in front of him and Jamie twisted onto his hip, face and shoulders leaning onto the window.

AJ's mother had not forgotten that the next door neighbor's daughter was turning thirteen, though she is still at work when he gets home. Set out on his bed is a hideous too-large jumper dress and an already-wrapped present.

Even if AJ wanted to wear girl's clothing, the things his mom picks out and mandates are humiliating. She still buys him little kid stuff in incrementally larger sizes, with no sense of context, telling him he looks "cute." The word "cute" feels like an insult for the rest of his life. He puts on the dress, and practically swims around in the garish materials.

It's no use arguing. His mother thinks his discomfort is an attempt to hurt her. He doesn't yet know most other children's parents do not physically restrain and slap them for wanting to dress themselves. This is how he started shoplifting in the first place. He wanted a denim jacket, unisex, well-fitting, so he nicked one from K-Mart. The desire was so practical, but it gave him something he never had before—a secret, a part of his life he could control.

The party invitations went to Crystal's actual friends, plus a pity list of neighbors and losers like AJ and Jamie. They were almost too old for this sort of forced mingling. In high school, AJ sensed, there'd be no pity list, which was almost a relief. But Jamie didn't seem to know that yet. He got an invitation to everybody's birthday, bar and bat mitzvah, and pool party since the fall. Eileen made sure he went to all of them.

AJ arrives early, in the ugly dress, mystery gift in hand, and fusses with his hair by the chip and dip table, then fusses with the food, fills his discomfort with Tostitos.

The trade-off Crystal had clearly negotiated with her parents was that if randos had to come, then her chosen few got to be co-ed, too. Her boyfriend Derek is there with the rest of his lacrosse team.

The atmosphere is relaxed—the "fire drill" had made the Friday especially casual and Crystal herself isn't a status conscious girl, just eager to please people like Derek, who most certainly is.

AJ blends into the shadows of the evening, melts into the wallpaper and the carpet, lurks by the French doors leading out to the patio of the Sazerac's back yard which abuts his own. Mrs. Sazerac's daffodil buds spear out of the garden on the edge of the property line. He watches the deep dark of the suburban night saturate the lawns, the daffodils, the patio.

Jamie arrives just as the conversation turns into a game of truth or dare. He's gel-spiked his hair, has too much cologne on, carries a distinct turquoise gift box. AJ recognizes it from the window displays of the Tiffany's shop at the mall. By the size, it has to be the silver heart pendant, easily the most popular piece of jewelry among the rich girls at school since the end of Winter break, when they conspicuously appeared around the delicate necks and wrists of blossoming princessettes. Getting one from a boyfriend, much less a boy at your birthday party, was unheard of.

"Hey, you look pretty," Jamie says to AJ as he approaches AJ's spot by the patio doors. AJ squirms.

"Jamie, that's…" AJ says, pointing an accusatory finger at the gift box. "She's gonna know you stole it, and Derek is going to beat the shit out of you."

"How do you know what it is?"

"Jaim, you can't give her that. It's like a step below a promise ring."

Jamie defensively pockets the box.

"Yeah Jaim," Derek snorts. He slithers over to the boys, but seemingly hasn't overheard their argument. "You smell like a hooker."

Derek punches Jamie in the arm, but sniffs him again. Crystal is engrossed in truth or dare across the room, and doesn't notice either Jamie's entrance or Derek's comment.

"Leave him alone, Derek," AJ says. Derek stares down AJ with sparks of unhinged loathing.

"I don't need you to fight for me," Jamie snaps at AJ. Derek is a bully but at least that script is safer than letting a mouthy tomboy stick up for him in the middle of their own argument.

"Look fag," Derek digs in. "You're only here because everyone feels bad about your stupid dad dying in Nine Eleven, but everybody fucking hates you and wishes you'd stop coming to the shit our moms make us invite you to. The two of you should stay home and pee in each other, see if it makes an ugly baby to keep you busy."

Jamie is silent and still. AJ's eyes well with tears, and he imagines himself gouging out Derek's eyes, twisting off his balls, anything, but he can barely stop his lip from quivering. He might like to kick Jamie in the shins, too.

"Oh my god, are you going to cry? Freaks." Derek rolls his eyes and rejoins the main group of the party. Crystal looks up and greets him with a smile, oblivious.

When they were very small, AJ and Crystal used to play Barbies together. They used to have fun. For some reason, this pops into AJ's mind as he chokes back sobs. With hands shaking, he grapples for the handle of the French doors and lets himself out onto the patio. After a stunned pause, Jamie follows.

AJ stares up at the light in the kitchen window of his own house next door. The light falls in long green stripes from the windows to the lawn, where it dissolves as the world between the houses tears itself apart. A new portal offers itself to the boys. A deeper sort of nothingness. Almost a void. In the dark, dark night outside, only they can see that the fabric of the veil is coming undone entirely.

Jamie steps up beside AJ.

"My mom is on a date tonight," he says.

"What?" AJ asks, barely able to listen to anything but the whistle of the growing tear in reality.

"I said my mom has a date tonight. She's out with a guy." Jamie takes the Tiffany's box back out of his coat pocket and fidgets with it.

"Oh," AJ responds, watching the world crumble around them. The portal swallows the daffodil garden and envelops them both, taking them somewhere else, as yet indiscernible, but solid, hot, windy, and hard underfoot.

"You can't—" AJ argues with the sound of the pendant rattling inside the box. "You can't just give people really nice things like that. It's too much."

AJ waits for a response, and it doesn't even have to be an apology, but there's only the knock of the silver against the cardboard, and the howl of the empty hole, now draping heavy around them, mending itself, leaving them alone together at their destination.

THE HEAVY THINGS

I got my period young, and heavy. Heavier than the health class pamphlet said it should be. When it came for the first time, I felt something prickling parts of me I'd never seen, and had been told never to touch.

In the elementary school bathroom, I tried to clean myself up with all of the paper towels I could grab, but I was frightened and clumsy. I cut my finger on something down there, the prickling thing. I was not the most hygienic kid and thought maybe it was a woodchip from the playground, somehow. I pried and found it again, and pulled. Out came a small sewing needle. The eye was barely wide enough for the finest thread, but it was unmistakable.

I suspected there were things we weren't learning from our health pamphlets, and wondered if this was one of them. By middle school, there were bigger needles, and small keys, and decorative screws, and the tiniest little pair of scissors, like something you'd get for a doll.

I told no one about what was happening with my body, and I certainly didn't ask if it was happening to theirs. School offered few answers. In biology class, I learned about eggs and sperm like they were tidal creatures outside ourselves, fascinating and mysterious but alien. In gym, the teacher told us about wearing deodorant and eating vegetables. She said it was cool and okay to be a virgin and everybody giggled.

Then the nurse and the guidance counselors took us into a special assembly where my options became more clear. We watched a half-melted old tape of a made-for-TV movie about a girl who wants to fit in at school so she stops eating to be skinny, and all her hair falls out and she feels awful, but along with everything else, her period stops coming. I had no idea such a thing was possible.

When I was older, I got myself to a doctor. I filled out a form that asked me about my cycle. I wrote down the dates of my last three, and noted that they had been a nail clipper, a construction screw, and a hex key. I asked the doctor about inducing amenorrhea. I said it just like that to sound medically informed. She frowned and looked at the clock on the wall.

The doctor admitted there were hormonal suppressants safer than an eating disorder. There was a white pill that I could take every day but it would make me much fatter and it might make me cry. There was a yellow shot I could take every week but it would make me much hairier and I might stop crying altogether. She presented both options as hopeless, because if I changed my mind, I'd be permanently fatter or hairier, by which she meant uglier, which even doctors equated with unhealthy.

I picked the yellow shot, though it took three hours to convince her. I said I'd starve myself otherwise and then the harm would be her fault. But I left with my prescription and I grew thick, beautiful hair all over my body and gained some lovely weight anyway and tools stopped growing and shedding from my uterine lining.

I was happier, until things changed in the world and medicine got expensive and hard to find and the sliding-scale clinics closed. I knew someone who could get me something under the table, but it would take a while. It would take too long, I felt, but I'd have to wait.

When my period came back, it was worse than before. I doubled over, confined to my bed with cramps for days, ruining all my sheets. I felt the sharp end of a screwdriver pushing down and out between my thighs. I dragged myself to the bathroom, and pulled down my sick day sweatpants and old boxers. The screwdriver handle was still partially wedged into my cervix, and pinching hard. I plucked out the useless, over-saturated tampon blocking it and felt around inside for a grip on the thing until, humming to myself between Hallelujah breaths, I yanked it out. I rinsed it off and looked it over as I washed my thighs and hands. It was a Phillips head.

Reluctantly, I begged my parents for help. Just a little money to get that under-the-table connection to work faster.

My mother said she and my father would always take care of me in my time of need. They paid for lunch and she suggested I go off my shots for a while, anyway. She said I should give my body a break.

I said it did not work like that. I didn't need to detox. She shook her head, said she was just worried about me. Said it was a mean world out there. Asked me what the long-term effects of the drugs were, anyway?

I pointed at dad, at his bald head and his beard. I said that's what the long-term effects are. I asked if she would give her body a rest from her heart medication. She shook her head again. It was hard for them to look at me.

Desperate, I finally told them about the screwdriver, and the years of nails and scissors and needles and keys, and how they were getting larger. I thought, if nothing else, they'd see the simple benefit of relieving me of this. They appeared to be listening. They looked at each other with serious faces and then at me with serious faces.

You know, my father idled aloud, it was your grandmother who had all the gadgets in the house when I was growing up. She found it very empowering.

My mother smiled. They can be very expensive, she nodded, as if in agreement. Do you think, she asked, you might be able to get a cordless drill or a nice knife set in time for Christmas?

THE SEED AND THE STONE

The Arbor tells us stories of a time before, when all the dead were kept in orchards that rolled endlessly, and had always been there, and people tended to them constantly in gratitude and respect for their ancestors. All the children in the Arboretum are packed into the seed bank, then filed along to the press room where a circle of granite the size of five of me is lowered down on bushels of apples. The sticky tang of fresh cider stings my nose.

I am ten years old and I ask him how it could be possible for orchards to be endless. He is annoyed but clearly does not expect someone so young to understand infinity and eternity, much less gratitude or respect. But I know how many hours go into tending fruit trees, because I have so many ancestors with their pears and apples coming in that autumn, and I've pruned and harvested as much as my calloused little hands could manage. Nothing simply appears, I insist, it must be cultivated. I picked a lot of those apples right there, I add. The Arbor sends me home early, tells me if I'm old enough to make cider and know so much about it, well then I'm old enough to drink it and learn for myself.

My Pah is in his last week of life and jokes that he might become something unobtrusive like a potted fern. My Dah is not having it. Dah would like Pah to decide for himself, but also in a way that Dah is comfortable with.

I am sixteen years old and I tell my Pah that I'll do the opposite, become an enormous maple tree who can only be reached with laborious care, tapped at just the right time in just the right conditions, gallons and gallons of my sap boiled down by my descendants who'll get only a small bottle of my smoky blessings. My Pah and I laugh together.

Dah is cross at both of us, the only one in the room taking our customs seriously. He says, don't you remember what our people have been through? Our struggle, our persecution, how few our numbers?

I say it's just a joke, because I'm not going to have any descendants, anyway. Dah slaps me and sends me out of the room.

From the hall I hear Pah and Dah's muffled scolding and pleading. Pah relents, kisses Dah, says he chooses red plum. He dies a few days later. Dah never apologizes for slapping me, never mentions it again. We visit the Arbor and receive the juvenile plum tree and I mouth every word of the ceremony as the Arbor drones through it, and we plant the delicate roots in Pah's ashes in a cramped plot of our overburdened orchards.

I'm hiding and sulking in the root cellar. I'm twenty-eight years old and have stormed out of a screaming match with Dah. I have failed to make children. Be like the seed of the fruit, says the Arbor; go forth and multiply. Be like the stone of the press; meld the fruit of each to the benefit of all. No one is the least concerned for my happiness. I must do this for the community.

It's not enough that I've kept to the rest of our practices, that I faithfully attend to the ancestors when so many of my peers have left, more each year, assimilating into that other society where they make children with their bodies like animals. Their animal children know nothing of our secrets.

I simply ask other questions of my ancestors. I press other kinds of ciders, wines, pickles, preserves.

In the cellar, I pry open a plum wine and drink about half the bottle. The drink makes me peckish so I open two or three jars of syruped pear, dried apples, jellied melon, and fermented radish. The fruit of the prophets and teachers and neighbors and witnesses and gossips that I devour disintegrates in my mouth, my stomach, my guts. My dilemma digests and I want to vomit, but I lay down and keep still with a tight throat. I need to understand, no matter how repulsive the ingredients.

I listen.

I learn that my parents tried for another child before me, but Dah over-fermented the brew and spoiled the whole batch.

I learn that Pah and Dah became strangers for some time after, and Pah brewed me on his own.

I learn that they reconciled when I was small, and Dah's seriousness was his commitment never to get distracted from the practices again, never to let our family spoil.

I gorge myself on the secrets of the dead late into the night and wake up in the cellar with a stomach distended and aching, but resolved. I have something special in mind for the stone, something I have pieced together from so many sweet and sour voices at once. I go back upstairs and approach my Dah, greet him gently, take his old hands, and propose another way.

I will arrange him his favorite dinner with a nectar that will turn him back into a child himself. A brew of my own recipe which fulfills the word of the custom, so that I might have made a child, and he might achieve a time before his sorrows, find his expectations for himself, and we could stay together always.

He agrees.

Everyone has what he wants. I am forty-one years old and keep the orchard grounds full-time. I live in the two room cabin by the edge of the pears. My specialty is fermentation. Dah lives with me, but we keep a certain privacy from one another, and it feels the most like trust that we've ever had. Dah is the Arbor's favorite acolyte, a dutiful scholar of the seed and the stone. He's small and agile now, too, so I send him up Pah's towering plum tree to pluck the fruit from the very top and down into our baskets. This year we have such an abundance that I can imagine an infinite yield in an eternal harvest. Each ripe little orb looks like a sunset hurling down to the ground, a tiny mystical vision I can hold in my palm.

WE DID NOT KNOW
WE WERE GIANTS

I saw the god of storms on the midsummer at the summit of my childhood. In bright, blessed solitude, high atop our mountain, I scoured for ground cherries along the ledge of an unshaded cliff. They grew within a crinkled husk, and when they ripened, the husks parted like eyelids and the sun-yellow fruit peered out like the jaundiced doubt of the elders. I plucked the delicate fruit out from the granite in fistfuls.

The rock crackled with current. I tasted the charge upon my lips and tongue, and beneath my arms, and along the sweat of my spine. The downy wisps of hair on my body stiffened sharp as thorns. The ground cherries glowed, and the pine needles sparked, and their roots surged and hummed. From my vantage, I turned and saw him as he strode the bouldered slopes between the trees. And from the brightness of him, from his presence, the storm came.

He was a great stag, so pale as the fog that white clouds gathered like a holy veil over the mountain. His hooves rolled heavy with thunder that boomed and crashed like an avalanche, thunder that coiled in the stomach before it echoed in the ears. Wheels of wind and quenches of rain poured along his path.

Behold, behold! It seemed all that I could say to witness him. His crown of antlers were blue-white and luminous bolts of lightning, and each sway of his head commanded a brilliant strike of that power, and he commanded that it upon the cliffside where there it struck through me and into the parched land. I cried out, and it was all that I could do to make that place sacred.

Does your country have such gods as these? Tell me, stranger, do you see them? Do they come to your land steady, or fickle? Do they bless you with bounty and miracles? Or do they scorch your prairies with their gales and fire, or churn your waters with their rapids and their undertow?

What, stranger, do you forfeit to endure them? Each midwinter beneath the hunger moon, my lanspeople sacrificed what little we had left to the gods that roamed our timbered mountains. They are mountains that rise from course and endless flats of pine barren. They are barrens that flow with tick-ridden and swamp-bottom sands.

We relished glimpses of our god-beasts and were grateful. The god of night emerged at dusk, a cautious black rabbit. At dawn, she dashed and hid from the god of day, that ferocious golden weasel in constant hunt of her. Do you see the flash of dark fur at the corners of the sunrise? We asked each other in greeting. We gestured with a pinch over our hearts, released over our shoulders. Did you catch the glorious sight of a shining tooth? We set aside a bit of our hunts and forages, a bit of our pride and sentiment, with the turn of each new day and each new year.

Our mountain concedes survival only to the hearty, to life that is willing and able to yield to her in return.

I returned from the cliffside unharmed by his lightning. I returned to our lodge purified by the splendor of it. We filled our barrels with his rains and rejoiced.

That year, the roots and leaves and fruits and seeds were great and many. The deer grew fat and careless. At frost, we stalked them by endurance and cut their exhausted throats. The shining quartz of our blades ran red as we sawed their flesh. We roasted it plain over fire, dried it spiced over smoke, pressed it with birch bark and buried it to ferment. Though no matter how easy or plentiful the game surrendered, no matter how we seasoned or prepared their carcasses, the meat of our mountain always tasted as bitter as the resin of the pines.

At midwinter, we brewed teas of mountainsweet and carried steaming mugs of it in our fur-wrapped hands. We made our procession through the forest, singing. All the land slept but the evergreens, our eternal giants, the steady fingers of the mountain herself. So as we kept wake and watch alongside them through the longest night, our song rose to meet the snowfall, and our voices rang across the frozen ground.

The hunger moon rose and we each proclaimed what precious

thing or attachment we renounced in the name of the coming year, in the name of survival. The cold pine wind stung our nostrils and nipped the wet of our eyes. At my turn, with a piety as clean as frost, I sacrificed everything that I still possessed.

First I gave up my pinewood baubles, and the elders called me faithful. My toys had splintered and scuffed my small hands, but I took comfort in their companionship.

Second I offered up my long-grown hair, and the elders called me passionate. My hair was as thin as the air and course as the brush, but I took pride in its plenty.

Last I renounced my given name, and the elders called me foolish. They called me knot-hearted. They said I would not attract special concern or praise through grand gestures. They warned me of youthful fits and folly, of making an indulgence out of denial, of narrowing the purpose of my life like the dark mouth of a cave.

The given name shimmered in my mind. I took pleasure in the sound of it when spoken. I cannot tell it to you, though it is no secret, and I have no more use for such luxury as secrets. After their warnings, I ceded it still.

I told the elders how the name kept me frivolous and vain, how being at all distinguished from others, distinguished from dirt, enabled intimacies and stoked desires, when I had been struck through with his lightning directly, when truly I had been called to serve, to give.

So I became nameless and was hollow, for the privilege of that lacking, for the emptiness of me. I prayed for my lanspeople, and for the thaw, and for the forest, and for the rains from the fog-white god of storms.

Most of all I prayed for him. For was he not the greatest light in the woods, in the world? The weasel's sun and the rabbit's moon surpassed the reach of our mountain, but his lightning relinquished jagged shards of the greedy sky to the humble ground. In what other being was such power tangible, terrestrialized?

The next year followed, and the red hawk delivered the first warm breath of thaw. Then the green beetle turned and resurrected the mulch. Streams of snowmelt gushed, but the rain did not come, and the streams soon trickled to creaks of dust, pebble, and filth. That year, the god of storms did not come at all.

The bottoms of our barrels cracked, their gaping mouths craned toward a cloudless sky. By midsummer, the leaves and flowers shriveled, and their roots burned, and what few cones dropped from the pines opened seedless. The deer did not calf, or give milk, and they collapsed in pestiliance instead of hunt. We found only putrid carcasses, overtaken with slow and delirious flies, pulling weak chews from brittle bones.

The mountain takes us all to death by some manner or by some means, and when she takes us, we lay our dead beneath her caustic soil. She takes by age, by sickness, by injury, by exposure. In that rainless heat, she raised her fists of drought and famine, and crushed near all our numbers in her burning palms.

It was a clear and snowless winter. There were no steaming mugs of mountainsweet. There was no procession and no songs. Those of us left huddled in our lodge around a meager fire. Quarreling with one another made for better warmth than the flames. We had never known such thirst until that year without the fog-white god, without the clouds and wind and rain and snow.

One elder said that we had been abandoned by him. What offense had we committed?

Another elder said that we had been forgotten by him. Should we not, in turn, forget as well?

I wondered if we had taken him for granted. I said that we must give more yet. Had we truly nothing left to sacrifice?

The first elder scowled at me and said I, alone, had over-given. Perhaps I, alone, was at fault. Was it not my zealotry that preceded the mountain falling out of balance? Had not I bragged and boasted of my special witness and duty to him?

The second elder, listening to this, turned toward me. Perhaps I, alone, was meant to be this next great sacrifice? Perhaps I, alone, should leave them, should wander the mountain in search of my beloved god, should repent before his presence with my own throat? The elders offered me this or, they agreed, they would slaughter me themselves.

I set into the darkness shaking, white grip upon the stone of my knife. I carried no warmth or rations, but what need of them had I? All my purpose then was my own annihilation. I moved at first by the silver columns of moonlight between the heavy pines, until I saw the faintest pulse of a spark along a fascicle of dry needles, and followed a lingering charge, descending the whole of the night, to the swamp-bottom of the pine barrens.

Distant there came a crack and a rustle, and the needles of the knobby scrub pines hummed and glowed. The hum grew to a dirge as I crept low as the beetle and quick as the rabbit. Nearing dawn, when the moon had set, there was no other light in all the world but the brightness that I longed for, the god that I pursued, the one I stalked and discovered far, far from our hearth.

He rested in dry, dead reeds and tall brown husks of grass, and arcs of lightning struck thinner than a spider's thread between his antlers, and bolted from the branches of his antlers to the branches of the trees, and through the trees to the ground. I approached him, and kneeled before him, and held my knife to my throat.

His great black eyes met my own, and it was as if he struck me with his lightning once again. I lightly drew my blade across my neck, enough to let the heat of my blood seep forth like the sap of a birch. Would it please him? I begged. Would he take my very life, that final lacking, for the rain?

I made myself as soft and still as solitude, patient as he watched me a long time. A fear ascended my spine. I noticed, at last, how deep was the cold. He looked down and chewed at the rind of a long-fallen pinecone. And I saw him as he truly was at last.

He was as indifferent as he was all mighty. His power was feral, knew and thought nothing of our great balance, of our bargains, our sacrifices, the reason or fairness of the mountain. That he had not come our way that year was as inscrutable as it was devastating.

I moved my knife from my throat to my heart, then, so that I might still cry out at the moment of my death, cry out that I despised him, and that I loved him, and that I repented in dust and ashes for however I had wronged him. Yet as I raised my voice to the empty black night, the forest behind us and beyond us stirred. And there came forth my every lansperson, surrounding in a circle, and raised up in arms. And fury, fury gleamed in the polish of their blades.

An elder whispered that I, alone, would not be enough, after all.

They had discussed the matter. They had tracked me all this way, all this night. They goaded me, not to efface my pitiful life, but that which I truly cherished most. And was it not the god that I loved most, so clearly surpassing even the love for my own life?

By their trembling, I knew what act I must carry out, but also that I would not act alone.

I praised the god once more, and said before my lanspeople that no longer did it matter if he loved us in return. That he was all mighty, that he held such power at all, was reason enough to destroy him.

I turned my knife away from my chest and towards the fog-white god, and my lanspeople took me into their fold, and we closed our flanks into a shining ring around him, like a crown of many stones inlaid within a single will. And we stepped forward on the bleakest valley of our land toward his fog-white hide. And we took him to slaughter, and we sang.

We carried the body of the god of storms up the mountain. We moved in slow procession, frozen, weary, raising lamentations. For we loved him most of all on that morning. We hung his carcass high outside the lodge, and tied him and drained him and drew his pooling blood across our foreheads, and blessed our youth with it.

There is meat enough for all to grow strong and fat. There is meat enough to store and smoke and ferment, to last us well through midsummer and the next longest night. We savor each morsel and wonder what, now, will bring the storms?

Might they never come, or might we become the ones to bring them? Might they no longer be tied to any force but their own? Have we become him, or have we destroyed the need for him?

We stoke the fires and chew at the marrow and sing to our youth. Once, the song goes, we were giants, but we did not know we were giants until we felled a god.

What are the certainties of your lands, stranger? We wish to learn. What questions would you ask of it? And would it answer you, and on what terms?

Do your young thrive and grow strong in the wilds? Do your people raise their voices to the clouds and cover themselves with a flood of water? Do they send the lightning bolts on their way?

Do you hear our hundred songs in the recitation of these words? Have you hospitality to grant our messengers? They have committed our questions to memory. They have raced to the gate and ground of your country to meet you. Do you hear us ringing out as one voice through their voices? Will you give them your answers? Will you permit them safe passage to return?

Do you hunt the gods of your country, stranger? Or do they prey upon you, neighbor, friend? If you slay them as we have slain ours, and if you eat them as we eat ours, I beg, describe to me the taste? I, alone, request this knowledge, as I eat my fill from the great abundance of his body, and my nameless flesh takes repossession of its power, chew by swallow.

I will tell you this. The flavor is as bright as lightning. It is as rich as thunder. It is as sweet as rain.

THE ANDROID THAT
DESIGNED ITSELF

I. SERMON FOR MY FABRICATED BODY

Why does God create grapes and wheat, but not wine and bread?
God does this because God wants us to share in the act of creation.
To be how you made me, to become how God made me, through
you, I can remake myself. You and I: we are already only whole, and
shifting towards the divine.

II. MANIFESTO FOR MY FABRICATED BODY

Make me two feet tall with fourteen arms, no legs, and a prehensile tail. Make me large and soft and rolling: a photovoltaic mucus that envelopes all it touches. Make me edible but make me poisonous. Give me one of every face that has ever been called ugly. Give me one of every skin that has ever been called excessive. Give me a way of moving that no space can admit or accommodate, and then reshape the entire world to hold me. Give me a sex that has never been seen before and a soft outline exactly the size and shape of my lovers, and when they lay their entire selves within it, that is how we are going to fuck, since you keep asking, and everybody wants to know.

III. THEORY FOR MY FABRICATED BODY

To take shape is to sever the infinite possibilities of wanting into a fragile burden of being. There is no guarantee this endeavor will yield anything but disappointment, and so there is a dread within the limitations. There is a question within the dread: what if I come to resent having changed myself, having become myself, for any reason at all? It is a dangerous, ridiculous, and insatiable curiosity. It is the only concrete act to save my own life. My life, which is worth more than the probability of outcomes, is greater than the sum and synthesis of its parts, so I am no longer afraid. My life, which is worth more than anyone's wanting, including your own, is not diminished by its smallness, but honed.

AS TENDER FEET OF CRETAN GIRLS DANCED ONCE AROUND AN ALTAR OF LOVE

I watch the dawn and her fingertips of rose unravel on the morning, the whole mile-wide sky like skeins fresh from the dyes of the madder root, while I stand with my toes curled over the concrete cliffs. They are cracked and slick with clinging seaweed and shell creatures and dark mold from the ocean below.

I spread a tincture of whipthorn blended with my own venom along the inside of my mouth and under my tongue especially, counting my breaths backwards as my nerves open wide, peering down the arid possibilities of the day, awaiting Her vision, teeming, impetuous.

I am undressed but it won't matter soon enough, and besides, this era has retained its wise and founded fear of nude women appearing beside bodies of water, even ones as ancient and ugly as myself. I am a known omen not to be disturbed.

Five days ago, I took down the poster tacked above my desk of one of Giorgio de Chirico's hundreds of Ariadne scenes. It had warped beyond appreciation. The blank building in which I lived and sold books had finally consumed the blank building within the picture. An arrangement of bare concrete has no business calling itself a dwelling anywhere with humidity, really. The walls in the house wept like a sacred image in the January moisture. The fog rolled off the Atlantic in the morning and lingered until supper, curling and corrupting my books like a tourist, and it didn't even buy anything when it left.

Tourists did find me occasionally, when they were lost. Because the Azores are islands, visitors from elsewhere bring their colonial imaginations with them. The pastures of cattle, the pineapple plantations, the last tea field, and the taro root sprouting along the hot springs are all very much souvenirs of empire on the once bald archipelago. From downtown Ponta Delgada, tourists skimmed a map and saw that my jetty was a short walk past where the docks end. They hoped, because they were on vacation and this entitled them to fancy, that it was a sandy beach. Most Azorean coastline is, rather, rocky cliff and sea wall constructed from the same crumbling industrial conglomerate as my little home. It's a different, thoroughly modern cousin to the mortars and cements we knew.

I believed a city that much more beautiful and enduring for the miracle of hydraulic limestone and those steadfast decorative flourishes of plaster fresco. I was intrigued by the process, by architects adding hair and blood and ash to improve the mixture.

And then, one hundred years ago, I watched an Englishman dissect a hilltop in our homeland and use the modern Portland concrete, reinforced with steel, to invent an elaborate structure on the site of our fabled lives. He built from his own designs and called it genuine, called it a resurrection, and sold the present as the past. As our past. Now I see his smug, unbaked loaf of a face in every building in every state of upkeep or neglect made of slurried stone.

Four days ago, I walked downtown to check my post office box. I set out in the midmorning during a drizzle of rain and passed the few other features on my jetty besides my home: a nightclub, a utility shed, and the great howling void of the ocean—sudden, mean, freezing cold, and gray as a callus.

As I approached the old part of the city, the streets and sidewalks transitioned from pavement to mosaics of black volcanic stone and white tile. I made my way along a sidewalk of pineapples and into a public square with a grand fountain. Nearby, an ornate wall, white with intertwining motifs of red flowers and gold stars. Then, the sloping, fading remains of an empty mansion, its grand gates and fences rusted and thick with the debris of abandoned fruit trees and untended gardens.

The white tile had become slippery in the rain. Along a side street embellished with wave and diamond shapes, I lost my balance. I fell to the ground face first, hands and knees out, and managed to bang up most of my joints and scrape my forehead. My reflexes are usually better, but this body was getting overripe.

The owner of a cafe, right across from where I lay heaped, darted out into the street and helped me to my feet. Finding no serious injury, he introduced himself as Dimas. He beckoned me inside, towards the warmth of the kitchen emanating over the lunch counter and two small tables. Seeing dry seats and smelling espresso, I nodded, muttering "Thank you, thank you," with some disorientation.

Dimas had the television above the bar on the news. An elected leader solemnly encouraged people looking for work to simply leave the country. As Dimas dished me beef stew and bread and coffee, he told me about his daughter who had done just this.

"She moved to Somerville. Do you know Somerville?"

I said I didn't. He explained it was in Massachusetts, in America, and there was a big Azorean population there already. He asked me if I understood and I said yes. He complimented my command of Portuguese despite my accent. Then he showed me a recent photo of his daughter, smiling and holding a tiny baby.

"I want to close this shop and move closer to my grandchild," he explained. "But I don't speak much English. I'll be a burden on my daughter. She said that Americans expect their coffee to be made by young people. Who would hire an old fart like me? What would I do with myself?"

"You could retire, and stay home with the baby," I suggested, "so she can work."

A long silence followed. I could see an awkward regret in his body language, maybe all the days of his daughter's own infancy or childhood that he'd been absent. There was something he could not excuse himself for.

"I hadn't thought of that," he said finally. I nodded, pretending that I had been minding my own business. I finished my food and drink, thanked him again, and excused myself.

Finally, I made it the remaining blocks to the post office and checked my mailbox. Small packages, solicitations, and a letter. I shuffled home to read them.

Kitane wrote that she'd received a vision of a red cyprus doorway. This time she would not reincarnate in the particular tradition of us snake women. This time she would pass through it willingly.

She also attached a new version of that story about you and your father and his white bull and the Athenian boy you're always associated with, for my collection. I set the clipping aside and I sat down in my molting armchair in the corner of my empty book shop, watching the softcovers crinkle like delicate mushrooms.

With Kitane done, there are no more snake women but me, Ariadne. That is, unless you are somehow alive. How to find you, if you're there at all? What charm or lure exists in all my fumbling powers? You are not in a place like these buildings are in a place. You are veiled by my grief, so obvious by these letters I cannot send.

I don't agonize about eternity much. I just want my friends back.

Three days ago, I cleaned my desk in preparation for my own reincarnation. My collection of Ariadne stories, like the one Kitane sent me, were tagged, alphabetized, and annotated in the drawers. There's a hundred true versions of what happened to you, and to us, and a thousand interestingly untrue versions, and a thousand-thousand uninteresting untrue versions.

But I am looking for your version, a closed text, a definitive narrative, though the Ariadne I knew as a girl would laugh at me for saying so. I'd ask you, were we friends or lovers? You'd answer, If I loved you, would it change anything? And so on until I'd beg you to decide your fate was with me.

Printing has allowed for canonization, which seems antithetical to the purpose of stories: things shared in context, much more about the teller, not dried out and hung up for solitary consideration. Still, I'm clearly not immune. I use the term "retelling" because of this enormous concern with authenticity, whatever that is.

Bookselling allows me to read widely and discover new instances of the telling of you, to feel something adjacent to love. Intimacy means something very different when you're three thousand years old and have outlived your own relevance. There is a trope in fictions. The lonely agony of the cursed immortal. An enchanted what's-it or who's-it keeps some fool alive forever more. I dislike these brooding characters and their clumsy symbolism. Somehow they're always frozen at their most sexually appealing.

No, no.

I relate much more to the white-knuckled shock of survivors. It's that feeling of having time but no future. The sense that you are part of an endangered species, but too frightened or bitter or numb or off your gourd to cooperate with the other rare beasts. So I seek out remainders and reminders, and take what I can get. An aftermath impersonating a woman, irreconcilably over-guarded and over-generous, and surrounded by citations.

I heard about a serious attempt to excavate the Labyrinth of Knossos over a century ago. I set out to a place they now called Crete, for the first time since I last saw you some three thousand years ago. I couldn't bring myself to try until then. I knew the place had seen a hundred other countries on its surface but this English archaeologist (wealthy grave robber) by the name of Sir Arthur Evans had specific interest in our country.

I stowed away on a supply ship and slept among crates of plum pudding, ox tongue, fruit salts, quinine, chocolate, and other repulsive English delicacies. When we arrived, I slithered away undetected. The first thing I did on land was take off my shoes.

I checked in for the long term at a crumbling rooming house. Visitors came and went as they pleased, without curfew, an informal brothel and drug den and place of worship and so much else. It reminded me of our Knossos, or my fantasy of our Knossos: the unraveled dream logic version conjured by three millennia of distance. I could feel the sea breeze in my bedroom with the windows locked and shuttered. At any hour I could hear women laughing, bickering, fucking, and singing. Wild flowers and sweet pipe tobacco helped mask the stench of rotting food and body odor.

That first night, I drank myself cross-eyed. I pulled at my hair and peeked out the window to watch the English soldiers and gentlemen, drunk and half out of their uniforms, come up to the side door of the building. They all had money in pocket, cigarette in mouth, and dick in hand, looking for the usual services.

I wondered if one might be Sir Arthur Evans, and if he might pay me for a fist fight instead. Violence can often suffice for closeness; I know this much about men. I reincarnate with whatever sex I see fit, and present myself according to whim as much as advantage, though what else I may be, I am always a snake woman in my practice.

I collapsed into the creaking bed frame and thin, grubby mattress. There was another occupied bed in the room. I blew out my candle and lay still, pretending not to notice she was too still and much too quiet to be asleep. In the pitch dark, I felt her watching me, letting her eyes fill up wide like ponds to receive and reflect me.

In the morning, I learned that Evans would pick his work crew at a local taverna, so I sought out the crowd. He hired both Christians and Muslims; that was his peacebuilding scheme. The solidarity, I suppose, of mutual exploitation.

The foreman rode up on his donkey, with Evans beside him on a horse. I made myself conspicuous. Someone's child starved for my determination, most certainly.

The foreman asked for diggers, and I showed him my hands. He scanned me with his animal eyes and asked how a woman came across hands like mine.

"A long, hard life," I snarled.

My hands have become massive and strange over the years. Every time I reincarnate, my face changes, my body reforms with its own nonlinear aging process, but it's like my hands are ingrown. They reform the same, only knottier at the joints and beefier in the palms.

The foreman went from squinting to flinching, but could not argue with the evidence, so I was chosen along with thirty others for an initial crew of diggers, shovelers, barrowmen, waterboys, and washerwomen. I was so obviously not from anyone's neighborhood. I am ugly and androgynous and intelligent. I am a beast. I intrigued the grave robbers. Evans himself stared at me.

I observed him in return as I walked behind the horse with the others to the site. From this I only gathered that he was not a patron of my boarding house. One invert knows another. What on earth would drive a person to excavate the ruins of someone else's country? What reason to scavenge bones? I couldn't get the image of a dirty, fractured skull out of my mind. I kept animating it backwards, putting the flesh back on, ringing out the dome with the bell of a living tongue.

I thought I might reclaim the graves before they were robbed. Then we arrived. Evans had a little tent set up for himself in the shade, complete with servants and a Union Jack on a flagpole. He was eager to have us get started. I was dizzy. I hadn't eaten.

I expected to recognize the curves of the land. I expected to recognize that place as though it were merely in disguise. I really, truly believed I would look at the dry hill and form special insights.

I took up a shovel. At the end of the first week, the crew had only unearthed dirt and a little recent garbage. I remember thinking about you when I looked into the holes I had dug, thinking I might find you there instead of shadows. I remember feeling that this made sense. I remember that it was very hot and bright outside, but that I shivered.

Somewhere, buried in the subterrane of my mind, is a perfect map of the Knossos complex and Labyrinth. Somewhere are the names of every snake woman, the details of my initiation rites, my own family, my childhood, your father, your mother, the Minotaur, the gods and the heroes and the fall, and you. I strain to retrieve them, surrender to them, but nothing surfaces.

Instead, I recall the voice of a landlady from three lifetimes ago with perfect clarity, a sound more smoke and phlegm than language. I recall the best octopus I ever tasted. I recall a lengthy book I read, and sold, and the customer who bought it; an orange I peeled; a war in Byzantium; a king in Egypt; all these cumulative sensations and experiences I've had since.

But when I search the time where you should be, there's response without action, tone without setting, mood without plot. All I possess of witnessing what happened to our lives and our love first hand is reflex and residue. Some days I forget to bathe and eat and sleep because I've been reminded of what I know but cannot think. I flinch, retreat within myself, lose time.

In my first thousand years, I was proud to have no trace of what must be shattering grief, a pride in what I thought was maturity, because I still did not yet understand that I am a great wounded bundle of coping mechanisms.

Then I thought I might cure my loss vicariously. I considered having children just long enough to wonder, envision, worry, despair, and discard the idea for the hundred fiftieth time. I've impregnated and been pregnant. Nothing seemed to take. I am outside the ability to place hope onto any other life.

I've known many children who grew up to maim and murder other people's children, without so much as eating the bodies. It's a senseless waste. People seem best equipped, historically, to breed tyrants. I am no different.

In those blackouts, those blank spaces, in the deepest base of my nature now, is but a pit of hungry serpents, eating their own young.

Two days ago, I dreamed about the poppy red yarn we dyed and wove with for our ceremonial skirts. We were good enough to turn sheep hair into something that draped around the moving body like flames. I saw after-images of the color as I dressed. I had a day or two, at the most, before it would be crucial to shed. Rain clouds loomed at the edge of the sky.

I hurried to the post office with my collection wrapped in two plastic shopping bags and tucked underneath my coat and against my chest. I would make copies of every entry, waterproof them, and mail them to trusted contacts in different corners of the world.

I passed by Dimas' cafe. He came rushing outside as though I might slip again on cue and placed his body squarely in my path.

"Miss Isadora, my friend," he addressed me, and I kept as neutral an expression as possible. If I lost my temper in public, I risked exposing my true nature to the town, and further complicating things.

"Mister Dimas," I responded, and stepped aside to keep going on my way.

"I enjoyed our conversation from before," he continued. "You are such a talented listener. I was wondering, I'm going to check on some business of mine near Furnas tomorrow. Do you want to come? There are two seats on my scooter."

"And why would I do this?"

"It's not bad alone," he said. "But it's better with company. We'd go along the coast and then up."

"I know the way to Furnas. I've walked it."

"It will be a treat then. The scenery is prettier when it goes by fast, but you'll want to wear gloves. It can get very cold."

If he threatened me, I would sink my teeth into his arteries and plunge venom into his veins and eat him whole. Maybe there would be a pit stop, a remote clearing, and I would obtain added energy for the tasks ahead of me.

"I suppose I have tomorrow free," I said, sizing up his culinary appeal.

"I am delighted to hear it." Dimas did look sincere. If it was a come-on or a trick it was a bold one. "I have a second helmet. And, you would have to hold onto me."

He held up both hands in surrender when he said this.

"I don't mind," I said to him. "Some fresh air could be invigorating."

"I will come pick you up," he said as I strode off, and I nodded without turning back around, set to obtain my mailing supplies, but he did not impede me any further that day.

Sir Arthur Evans moved the fruitless dig uphill after the first weeks, and we unearthed a plaza and a room around a set of alabaster stairs descending into it, with a chair and a basin carved right into the stone.

Evans would appear from his villa at the end of each day and stroll among our findings, personally burdened with returning significance to every ceramic sherd. We would all wait for him to do this, caked in dirt and sun-tired, our feet blistering and our backs sore.

When he surveyed the plaza and stood in the alabaster room, basking in his own genius, he burst forth with giddy congratulations to the whole crew. He announced that we had discovered "Ariadne's dancing floor" and "Ariadne's throne room." He mandated that we throw a festival. He meant to uncover, in our line dancing, residue of esoteric Minoan rituals. This was something the Cretan people, he believed, were too close in proximity to understand.

I barely restrained my impulse to eat him. I looked at this "dancing floor" and into this "throne room" and tried to remember the true layout and functions of our palace-temple. Every time I thought about it, the facts degraded.

An American filmmaker came to see "the real Labyrinth" and find inspiration within it, as so many artists did in those early years. He arrived with his arsenal of cameras, canisters, splicers, tape, assistants. My roommate took notice of him immediately. Her name was Eleni. I understood the trajectory of her ambition, and she begged me to attend the dances with her to catch his attention.

Eleni, her wide and quiet eyes in the dark, grew boisterous in the sun. I sensed she was new to being on her own and had important people looking for her. Whether this was a family, a fiancé, or a jailer was anyone's guess. She had a way of getting things for free without having to steal, a charisma I lack, and I respected how she wielded it. She could read and write and told me that she wanted, more than anything, to be an actress.

Hand in hand on the dancing floor, we leapt into the air and spun, coiling and circling each other but always returning to a circle. We were barefoot and spry, performing whole-body prayer, hers crying out. I was midair, upside down for the entire experience as far as I know, my sweat wicking away in the hot wind, my hair hanging down to the stone like an escape rope, my tender feet holding up the sun. The filmmaker was delighted. Evans beckoned us to return to the line and behave more authentically.

I fixated on uncovering my own knowledge of the space. I remembered remembering. The more I obsessed, the more copies-of-copies replaced my certainty, until I dissolved any chance at reclaiming that legendary hole in the ground.

I had come to Crete and joined the Evans excavation in order to lord my expertise over him, and pocket sacred objects before they could be whisked off to the Ashmolean. Instead, I spent half a lifetime wiping sweat from my forehead and rubbing the sting of dust from my eyes with my monstrous hands. I watched as this man redesigned the rubble he found into impossible, triple story complexes of poured concrete and "restored" frescoes—really images entirely of his own direction with the modern hand of a father and son painting team.

At least I got my fill of British soldiers now and then, swallowing the ones who gave my boarding mates more trouble than profit.

The filmmaker left one autumn with his exposed rolls, his dance studies, his arsenal, and Eleni. He did eventually make a film about your story. She played a beautiful and treacherous Ariadne, who meets a tragic end, captivating the collective hunger of the viewer to witness a sex object destroyed.

I suppose she eloped willingly, though we slept together once, at her suggestion, the night before she left. With every kiss and caress, the deeper I pressed into her, the further from me she became. Outwardly, she appeared satisfied and tenderized, though I seemed to be, above all, nullifying rather than answering some question for her. I understood that I was helping her to leave. This was a relief for me. My focus, my center of gravity, was elsewhere, too.

Yesterday, before dawn and all through the morning, I purged my facade of a home, my veneer of a shop, my suggestion of a life. My next dwelling might be a mud puddle, a hay pile, the bottom of the

Mariana Trench. Anything but that molding concrete bunker from this dying age.

I brewed a tincture of whipthorn and venom and set it aside to steep. By midday, little remained inside the building except my Ariadne collection, bundled neatly, transforming all those excerpts, fabrications, and forgeries into a sacred text.

What am I without them? Without you? What else but this graphomancy can reaffix my memory, can answer me when you do not?

I heard the putter of Dimas' scooter, approaching then idling outside. I threw on my coat, stormed outside, and climbed onto the back saddle of the canary yellow Vespa. We headed east along the coast, through the outskirts and into the pastures and villages. It was a cool, humid afternoon with plenty of wind even before we got up to top speed.

Some village houses were like my own. Others were bigger, older, had brick foundations and barn roofs. Most were a quick, uneven slab of material with a leaking roof. A building, even a hideous and clumsy one, expresses some kind of narrative, about the future as much as the past.

Dimas steered us inland, and I leaned my body with the turn and glanced as far behind me as I could. The dark ocean and the misty grounds of a church and monastery shrunk to a backdrop and then vanished. My knees ached from straddling the bike. The air whipped the warmth out of my hands and sound from my ears. I tentatively rested my chin and then my chest against the back of his hunched shoulders.

Lagoa do Fogo on the road to Furnas, in the heart of São Miguel, is a deep, marvelous cerulean lake nestled in a valley of volcanoes. The hot springs there are diverted along with a cold water source into a bathing park, and oxidized iron in the surrounding soil turns all of the water the color of spiced oranges. Buried pots of stew cook in the boiling mud. Dimas slowed along one side of the lake.

It hadn't occurred to me to ask what business exactly he had up here, especially in the off season. We continued on through the town, some woods, a field of sheep, and finally pulled over in front of a tiny parish and graveyard. The sun broke through the overcast haze as Dimas dismounted the scooter and approached a plot in the graveyard.

I hopped down and stretched my old bones and waited at a distance. Did he want me to hold some immaterial weight for him, or simply witness the state he was in?

"Miss Isadora," he began—so I stepped forward. "I'm moving to Massachusetts to live with my daughter, and I don't think I will have it in me to make visits back once I do. Not while I'm alive at least."

"Are you threatening to haunt me?" I teased.

"Definitely," he said. "Haunt, or send mail."

"Well, good luck with that. I am moving on as well, so your ghost will have to find me."

"Retiring too? Where is your family?"

I scratched at my arms and ashen scales flaked off. My skin was taut, itchy, gray.

"Mm," I shook my head. "No family anymore. I think."

"Not even a cousin's cousin?"

"I'm the very last one."

Dimas looked at me hard-lipped and aghast.

"How do you bear it?"

"Oh, so I should kill myself instead? No. I'm still learning to live well. Any thought of dying well is premature. Give me another thousand years, at least."

Give me until the sun swells to an angry, deadly red and swallows the whole planet.

Dimas gestured at the ground.

"This plot has my wife's family." He pointed to each marker. "Those two are her parents, there is her brother, and here she is."

"Saying goodbye?"

"No, apologizing."

"Oh, you pitiful creature." And I felt that immaterial weight of his after all and deliberated how to grapple with it. "You needed a confessor. This is why you asked me along, isn't it?"

"I cannot deny that is one way to see it."

"Then out with it."

"I was indifferent to my wife, and she knew it. I married her for her family, and nothing else. There."

"They were wealthy?"

"No. I was in love with her brother."

"Ah. Well." One invert knows another. "Did he love you back?"

"I don't know." Dimas stood in silence for a moment. "I had my one life with my wife and my daughter, and this other life with him. He would speak to me like a brother-in-law in every other setting, but say nothing at all when we were passionate. It was like he needed to keep his words and actions in separate worlds, just as I had to divide my own world between him and his sister."

I waited while he wept for several minutes.

"Am I a bad person, Isa? Am I a coward? What if I had

controlled myself? Been devoted to one or left them both?"

"And what if you had?" I snapped. He looked so pathetic, I salivated. "If I absolve you, can we leave? Would a different life resemble how you imagined it? Weren't you all cowards? Isn't the world ultimately hostile towards unmodeled happiness? Did anyone force your wife to marry you?"

"No ..." He said. "She wanted a baby. A daughter, in fact."

"Well?"

Dimas half nodded and half shrugged.

"Don't you ever wish you'd been just a little better, or more useful? Isn't there anyone you could have just been kinder to?"

I laughed with all the bitterness in me, Ariadne, which was hardly fair to Dimas. Yet, in the hideous release of that air, I jostled some small ache in the middle of my chest that had sat so long I hadn't realized I was carrying it anymore. All at once, there it was, come loose and rattling about in my ribs, hardening my throat and my humors and the very glands of my venom. It was a memory, forgotten, and then retrieved, and then it exploding in a great starburst of anger, so that like Dimas, I stood there, possessed and weeping.

You took me by the wrist, before I could scratch my tattoos again.

"Stop it," you whispered. "It's gross. Your arms will rot off."

Pasiphae had seen a vision and declared a state of waiting for King Minos to return after seven years of travel, trade, and pillage. We all stayed high above the docks, looking like a flock of harpies in our open bodices and poppy red skirts and capes, all those gold rings, bare feet and lean muscles from leaping over bulls for fun.

Pasiphae, the only one in murex-purple, stood on the walls at the far edge of the garden, cupped hands shading her eyes, fixed on the horizon for signs of the fleet.

"I'm not painted, I'm engraved," I whispered to you, waving my arms, and you laughed through your nose with a little snort. The gold pins fastening your hair glittered beneath the vines.

"I'm a cuneiform tablet," I continued. "I'm scrimshaw."

I wanted you to keep laughing, to never stop laughing, to exist forever in that half moment as a plump, happy girl with a clear purpose, with self possession.

Pasiphae shouted something I did not hear. We all gathered by the wall outside the shade and climbed it to look. Blue shadows bloomed around our feet in the late sun. We watched the ships arrive, and the dignitaries swarm to meet King Minos.

They were all Minos, him and his father and all of their fathers before that. Officially, there had only ever been one king, the same demigod reincarnated for the whole length of our national memory. I knew nothing of your family life yet. To be a princess seemed terribly glamorous, but there had never been an incarnation of Minos with an interest in his daughters. You came to the snake women the same as the rest of us, she-runts and step-children, unfit for marriage, obsessive, posturing, amoral.

Against the wash of battered bodies from the ship's galley, Minos conducted his procession in a black tunic, with a gigantic white bull on a chain at his side. He looked stark and infallible against the grizzle of his sailors and his slaves. The bull had aura of purpose behind its eyes. It looked right at us and I heard you gasp, and I felt you shiver, and you withdrew from the crowd to be alone. I scratched my arms, and they wept a yolky fluid.

Dimas and I ate lunch at a small restaurant in Furnas, and I saw on his crinkled face an expression of resolution where there had been agony just hours before. My hostility and cynicism must have read as intelligence and wisdom to his generous nature.

He smiled at the server with a mouth full of cake.

"This is the best food I have had in so long," he remarked, spraying wet crumbs on the table, the floor, himself, me.

It could be that simple for him, that elegant. But though I, too, felt the bleary release of a good cry, no comfort came. Unlike Dimas, I did not know who or what exactly my tears were for. The weight in me remained. I poked at the bun of my hamburger, wishing I had devoured the easy prey across from me before losing my appetite altogether. If my next life were to be any different, I thought, I would have to know a slaughter from a sacrifice. The change would have to be my own.

Oh, Ariadne.

You can grieve for the possible futures you eliminate by making an important choice, even when your choice is undoubted. Choosing is extremely powerful magic. Its power derives from the death of what is not chosen.

"As a practitioner," Pasiphae once told us, "do not take for granted that all power derives from death, unless you are a god— and you are not a god."

Dimas took my giant hands in his own. He said nothing of their size or deformity, nothing of the thick crust of dead skin loosening off them and ready to slough.

"Thank you, my friend, thank you," he said. "You have helped me."

"All I did was yell at you," I replied.

"Yes, yes," he said, nodding. "Thank you, again."

A sensation of pinpricks of crept throughout my belly.

Dimas insisted on paying for lunch, and drove us back into the city with his helmet visor up, singing tunelessly into the whiplash of cold air. He dropped me at the jetty.

Just before dawn, I undressed and walked outside to the edge of the water with my tincture and my collection. I set it down on the cliffside and imagined it an altar, then tore each one into ribbons and devoured every scrap. I cleansed my mouth with the whipthorn and venom.

The sky, sea, tiles, bricks, containments and remainders, bled away. For a moment I heard the faintest static of the crashing waves and the whistle of airplanes, and then I was elsewhere, elsewhen, beyond the veils of consensual reality.

A marble complex with twisting hallways and hidden passages. A pair of bovid horns, polished and hollow, with gilding over the serrations where they were sawed from the carrion of their owner. They are vessels resting on a pedestal painted with a motif of monsters. The monsters are dying or slain, but as if by sudden will. There's not a hero or a weapon among them.

I touch the horn-cups and the darkness brimming within them ripples. I bring one to my nose to discern the aroma. It is not sea water, or poison, or potion. It is not wine, or blood, or medicine.

I drink and find myself in another room. Everywhere around me are the cold bodies of the dead. They are a hundred fifty generations dense and piled atop one another, stored neatly like grain baskets and amphora. Their eyelids are open but their eyes have been replaced with orbs of copper, silver, gold, iron, stone, lapis lazuli, ruby, ivory. I look for you among them but I cannot find you there.

I do find Kitane and her blank expression, two perfect spheres of mercury.

"So soon?" I ask her, to no effect, of course.

I drink again and find myself in another room. Everywhere around me are the warm bodies of the living. They are consumed by their work. The weaver rips her yarn out and starts over, but she is smiling. The potter smashes his wares, the glaze still wet, and sets back down by his wheel with a gleam of mischief. An inventor turns out marvel after marvel and sets them aflame, laughing and prancing around each immolated genius. I look for you among them but I cannot find you there.

I drink again and find myself in Her incomprehensible presence. I cannot perceive Her, not yet, not until She wills it, but I feel Her dividing my existence. I refract into triplets, the sacred impulses of living, dying, and reproducing. There are no simple opposites, no dualism or dichotomy. Persisting consorts with negation and multitude. A white hot, piercing absence; a rich black mulch of abundance; a difficult prism of stasis.

My nerves burn, my blood boils, and my skin sweats and thickens. The horn-cup drops and I collapse. My organs liquefy and pool out from every orifice. My bones soften to jelly. My heart becomes a hard thing, like a tumor and then like a stone, until it bursts out of the limp hollow of my insides, and expands. It grows into a whole self. I am newly perpetuated, flush with blood and mucus. All is too loud and too bright. I am weak, except for my hands. With them, I cannibalize the sour remains of my old body for nourishment.

There in the acid of my former belly are all the tattered assertions about us, the chewed and distilled bits of myth from my collection. This world that keeps you alive assigns so much contradiction to you. A thousand-thousand iterations of Ariadne. How well I know each one. Ariadne is a painting, a poem, an opera, and a session of psychoanalysis. Ariadne is the dream of a foreign archeologist swallowed whole in his sleep by a monster. Ariadne is remembered by her sisters in ophidian sorcery. Ariadne is culpable for the fall of Knossos. Ariadne is mad with love. Ariadne is self-destructive. Ariadne is abandoned. Ariadne is unrecognizable. Ariadne is unmarried. Ariadne is a way of talking about the past. Ariadne is a way of talking about women. Ariadne is furious.

Have I not kept track of you well, my love? Or have I reduced you, just the same as countless others, by doing so?

In a moment I will return to that keeping world, renewed, reborn. The serpent is eternal and shrewd. The Goddess will grant me my new life, for the sacrifices I have made.

When She reveals Herself to me, She is towering and muscular and bare chested. A lioness sleeps in Her braided hair. A golden serpent winds around each long, bronze arm. She picks the horn-cup from the ground and holds it in one hand, like it were the the most delicate little thorn. In Her other hand, its twin, still brimming. Questions simmer in me. Questions rife with ingratitude and yearning froth forth in the vulgar limits of speech.

She smiles, and just to witness it, I am at once broken and in bloom. I weep and tremble at Her feet. I feel Her reassemble my existence, allow my feeble and repulsive reincarnation to return through the veil. Before I wake to an unfamiliar morning, I see only Her face. Her eyes are dark as caves, an endless and indescribable fecundity, the blackness that is beyond blackness. I look for you inside it but I cannot find you there.

ESTRANGED CHILDREN
OF STORYBOOK HOUSES

My brother thought that he might burn the fairy out of me when we were children. He had learned about them in school. Common wisdom held that a fairy would reveal itself if held to flames or iron. Then it would cry out in its own wicked tongues, leave the home it had invaded, and return the rightful child from its realm. My brother tested for my sinister nature with the hot end of a fireplace poker.

He said that I did cry out, and that I cursed in a funny language. Not a curse like a swear word. A curse like a wish against him, a wish that came true. I don't remember any magic words, or the shape of my mouth around them, or what they brought into being or unbeing for my brother, but there is a white welt on my chest where the skin curdled and rose up like cream.

"But you didn't even go back," he said. "You cheated."

He was only ten months older than me. "Irish twins." In most ways, I resembled the baby sister that our mother had delivered in the bathtub. Then at the age most children were eager to speak, I seldom did. While our classmates watched grown-ups intently, eager to imitate, eager to elicit reactions, my gaze wandered ever-elsewhere.

Briefly, our parents called me their little daydreamer, but at some point they stopped, and called my same behaviors inappropriate. They tried to help me understand when it was happening with a pinch on the arm, a slap across the ear, but I didn't learn right. It was between "daydreamer" and "inappropriate" that my brother grew suspicious, and tried the more traditional method.

It all must have been frightening for him. I commanded more and more of our parents time, necessitating more severe correction, more sustained attention. He had to be tough and brave and perfectly free to get into trouble when no one was looking, and no one was ever looking. He could stretch out his whims within red-blooded boyishness. He could adapt to suit a situation, and to get whatever it was that he wanted. The sheer limitlessness could have been overwhelming.

I got shuttled back and forth between special kinds of teachers and expensive doctors who instructed parents on how best to approach their changelings. I remember visits to a famous one, who had written a best-selling book, *Managing the Fairy in Your Family*. He had a voice full of warmth and optimism when he spoke to my parents about me, as though I were not in the room beside them.

"It's different in girls," he said. "But I believe we'll find the cure within her lifetime, and meanwhile!" He laughed like hot chocolate bubbles in a saucepot.

We were left alone for periods of time. I'm sure they were called therapeutic sessions, because I remember how seriously I was corrected when I once called them training. He squeezed my arms to my side and pulled my chin up towards his face.

"Look at me," he said, and smiled. I hated his touch, even though he had a grandfatherly lightness to his grip. The mild, old-fashioned smell of his aftershave was enough to set off a dizziness and nausea that lingered for the rest of any day I saw him. I squirmed, and he held tighter, and adjusted me again. "Look me in the eye."

By different experts, growing up, I was deemed gifted, disturbed, blessed, cursed, enlightened, feral, clairvoyant, and psychotic. My emotions were both stoic and oversized, my appearance both negligent and fussy, my body at once too bullish and too delicate. I have been a savant, a magician, and a mutant. I rarely knew which one it was until it shifted again.

Grief was the one constant around me. It was a grief that brought out my father's shyness and my mother's fear. They would call it other things, if they knew I'd named it grief. They would call it worry and love and looking-out-for and doing-right-by, but I understood how mourning folded into all of those. When I became an adult, it was decided for me that I was incapable of living on my own, and I understood that my needs were not needs like other adults, but tragedies to those around me.

I understood what they had worked so hard to teach me. A

changeling was a devastating loss to bear for any parent. A changeling was a queer and sickly substitute for the good and healthy child they had planned for and expected, the child that had been stolen from them.

When our mother lost her mobility and our father lost his speech, my brother came out from his big house in the city to oversee them and the daytime aides he hired.

"We're so lucky that he's done so well for himself," my mother said to me. "That he can take care of us all."

His pregnant wife would join us on weekends. Our little single-wide hardly fit the four, five, six, seven, or eight of us there at a given moment; the exterior encumbered with novelty patio decor, suncatchers, wind socks, bird houses, gingerbread trim; the interior over-full with dusty half-finished craft projects, collections of glass angels clutching glass infants, the accumulation of years of markdown bins at the checkout aisles of JoAnn's Fabrics. Everyone stepped over and around it and buzzed about our mother, who directed like a queen bee. If I cooked lunch or emptied the sink, inevitably someone shooed me away to do it themselves, even my swollen-foot sister-in-law and my mute father.

"If you want to help," my brother said. "Get out of the way."

One cold weekend, I sat hatless on the back steps while my father surveyed the retractions of snow around his garden. A home aide opened the kitchen window above the stove. Steam curled out. Conversation carried clear as ice.

"Well, I've researched a lot online and talked to so many other moms about it over the years," my mother whispered. "If it happens to yours, there's a great community of support. Of course, you love them no matter what. They're still your baby, in a way."

"Oh, of course," assured my brother. "I just wanted to know what you, personally, think causes it? It's not that I'd love my child any less, it's just, you know, if you could choose between one way or the other, if you could head it off… You'd want the easier path for your child, just as a parent."

"Are you planning to vaccinate? One of the women on the online chat was saying she thinks they elevate the risk, that the, um, the 'folk' can smell the chemicals."

"We're vaccinating." My sister-in-law interrupted her.

"Well, I suppose that's your right, but I wouldn't risk it, if I could do it again."

I pulled at the laces of my jacket. A fat brown woodchuck darted from the woods and into the opening of a burrow along the bottom of the shed. My father stood still and watched for more.

"At least that got rid of the rabbits like you wanted," I called to him. He turned to show me his frustration. If he heard the conversation from the kitchen, he was more focused on the burrows in the backyard.

My sister-in-law went back into the city for work in the morning. I went to my parent's room where they ate their toast and juice on trays in bed. My brother sat in their recliner with his coffee.

"I'm leaving to find your real daughter," I told them. "I'll un-trade places with her, or bring her back with me. This is how I can help."

My father blinked back tears. My mother reached for me and I went to her and received her embrace, cool and light as paper.

"I'm sorry," I told them. "I'm sorry I didn't think of it before." The daytime aide arrived to strip the beds and start the laundry. I started to add, "I wish I could wish it right," but my brother stood as if to intercept the words.

"Go on and go, then," he said, and urged me from the bedroom as though the sight of soiled sheets was forbidden, as though the smell might compel me to stay.

Behind the garden and the shade-choked lawn ran the edge of the wild woods coming into bud. I'd played in the woods countless times. They descended to a swamp and a kettle pond where I'd caught many handsome frogs. At the opposite shore was a hill and a flat and a neighbor's strawberry farm neatly outlined in low rock walls.

Common wisdom held that fairies were encountered at perimeters. I combined as many liminal conditions as I could, and crossed into the boundary of the woods at the sunrise between winter and spring while wearing a thick wool sweater and thin cotton shorts.

I pushed into tangled growth and hazy fog. Bushes and thorns scratched my legs. Something nipped at my knee and jolted away behind me. When I looked down and around, though, I was alone, and the path I'd cleared had regrown, replenished and green.

I followed. The trees blossomed around me as I moved, as though spring accelerated four and then six and then eight weeks further along than it was at home. I heard their music whistling from the flutes of ferns and the chimes of mushrooms. The moss sighed and the lichen hummed.

I followed. White crows fed tendrils of mist to their black-eyed hatchlings. The soft beaks of the baby birds gaped and gobbled at the slithering whisps. The light was not the sun's, not the light of any time of day or tilt of the hemisphere that I knew. It was more like the light I'd seen in movie theaters, when it flickers across a room that shuts out all else to hold space for illusions.

I followed. Their summer court was a sprawl of festivities and makeshift structures. I saw a thousand faces like faces I'd glimpsed in passing before. Their outfits were exquisite or nonexistent. I caught my breath. No one accosted or questioned me. I moved among them with the flow of the crowd, where there, easy as dreaming, I found her.

The one with the face like mine, I thought, before I shamefully remembered that I was the imitator, that I had come here at all to reconcile a great wrong evidenced by my false life. Common wisdom held that fairies were made of pure madness. She was the human child made of reason. I was merely a shadow or delusion poured into her absence.

I approached her. "I've lived as you, in your place, with your family," I said. "And you were so close this whole time?" My stomach turned. I could not have walked more than a mile or two, what would otherwise be square among the neighbor's strawberries.

She looked pleased, but unsurprised. "Well here you are now. Look at us, two corners of the same circle, together at last!"

I was sure I'd misunderstood her. "You're not upset?"

"Oh, that's not the word I'd use." She folded her arms across her bare chest. She was nude except for sunglasses and silver cowboy boots. "Do you really think all fairies and their people live just beyond your crab apples?"

She laughed and pointed across a courtyard, breaking into a stride and urging me to follow her through the revels.

"I guess there's no way it's that straightforward," I said, and jogged to keep up. "Our—your—parents miss you, though. Will you leave with me? To see them?"

"How could they miss me if they've never met me?" There was an open innocence to the way she asked me this. Her puzzlement seemed sincere.

"They love you," I said. "You've never wondered about them?"

We passed a scroll-legged table piled with pastries, and a fountain shaped like a laughing old woman. Bubbling wine sprayed out from the ends of her hanging stone breasts.

"Everyone here loves me, too." She shrugged. "I was very special and lucky to be chosen."

"You're brainwashed, then," I said.

"Nope! Just bragging. You know, you're bigger than I pictured you."

Even in boots, she was just a bit shorter than me. Otherwise, we appeared the same.

"I pictured you differently, too," I said. I had pictured her prettier and rosier but not so decadent. Smiling but not grinning so wide. "With, um, with more clothes on."

She laughed and continued to lead us out the other side of the crowds and festivities and toward a idyllic seclusion of huts, tents, trailers, and cabins that ran along a wide, misty cobblestone road leading out and onward. I thought she must be taking us a faster way home than I had come. My neck was hot in the sweater and my legs were cold in the shorts. My nose and throat itched from an unfamiliar pollen.

"You can borrow my sweater. For the visit, I mean. Or whatever you can to throw on. Your parents won't be picky about how you look, it would make them so happy just to see you."

"My parents, hm? Mother, father, brother, sister, family." She over-enunciated the words, rolling and stretching each syllable in her mouth like it were taffy. "Seems like some kind of weird blood cult. Since you mention brainwashing and all."

She stopped outside a single-room dwelling, and invited me inside. It was a cozy little cabin, flush with pillows and blankets and cushions, and long counter of snacks and stimulants.

"So you won't go back with me?"

"I don't see the point, really!" She pulled out bread and honey and cookies alongside fruit lozenges, colored powders, and a syrup that might just have been cough medicine. "Maybe another time. You've come much a longer way than you think. Why don't you stay and rest a while here?"

Time vanished in the summer court. Stars fell like snow and fluttered through the windows with the lightning bugs. The moon was always full and red-gold. My memory flowed away from me as easy as their wine poured from carafes that never emptied. No one seemed rooted to any sort of grand or personal past. Pains and grudges and judgement lifted off from every heart as light as birds.

They had neither knowledge or need of moderation, either. I spent most of my indistinguishable days and nights there overstimulated. I never did adapt to the pollen. I regressed to building blackout forts and quiet chambers out of the blankets, blowing my nose, and taking naps though I was never fully tired, either.

My memories of home faded and blurred, and with them, my sense of whatever it was I had come for. I had the loosest sense there was another, sharper place that I had come from, a place where many apologies were owed but everybody strutted around as though this ache were not their problem. I knew, however, that it was my problem. I forgot that I had ever lived anywhere else, but I remembered that somehow, somewhere, I'd failed.

On a twilight like every other dayless, nightless twilight in the court, my double readied for another wonderful ball or orgy or feast.

"I'm sorry I'm a wet blanket," I sniffled from under a pile of pillows.

"What a weird thing to apologize for!" she said.

"I don't do anything. All of you are so creative and fun, or just busy... happy..."

"Just you living and being here is so great." She wrapped herself in a cape of white crow feathers and snapped a glittering party hat onto her head, then blew me a kiss. "There's nothing wrong with you."

I clenched everywhere. My body remembered what my mind forgot.

"How could you say that?"

I told her that I was a parasite. I said: shadow, double, broken, fake, trick, broken, defect, mutant, broken. I said nobody wished for this, to be this. I said nobody wished for me. She asked me what, then, did they wish for?

I heaved. I told her that I had to go back home, wherever that was, and that I couldn't go back without her, but that I couldn't go back with her. I thought that she would be whole where I was deficient, but instead, she was all too much where I was too little. The child that our parents mourned resembled neither one of us.

We were like orphans. I could only invert one grief into another grief. I failed them either way.

"Maybe they're enchanted!" she said and clapped her hands. "And that's why they miss and expect and think they're owed this mysterious person who doesn't exist! You can't undo such a powerful spell for them, unfortunately. They'll have to take three jars of honey from the August Bees to the troll that they've offended, and then—"

I threw up inside the blanket fort.

"Uh-oh!" She laughed and rubbed my back, and it felt like being touched by my own hands. Safe. Not too much at all, not for me. We cleaned up the vomit together, and then she left me to wash up and wallow alone, and she continued out and onward, doing exactly as she pleased.

I ventured home alone. I thought I might have been away a week or two, but it had been years. The grass was high and wild. The golden heads of the dandelions had turned to clouds of seeded down that swayed in the breeze, ripe to burst in the next gust of wind.

I never understood why they had to get cut. I would ask my father, why not just let them grow? He'd point out a patch overtaking some corner of the lawn or the garden.

"Do you see all the other plants doing so well beside them?" He would say. There were none, of course. The dandelions choked them out to proliferate. "See, they're only weeds." Then he would push out the lawn mower.

I threw tantrums about this. I hated the grinding sound of the motor and the way the cut scent of the lawn that everyone else found so pleasant was, to me, so clearly an odor of distress. The grass and the dandelions screamed in their own way, so I screamed in mine. Most times my father ignored this.

"I've already explained it to you," he would say. Once in a while, though, I would later discover a bouquet in my room. A clean jelly jar stuffed with yellow dandelions, cut as though they were roses.

I knocked at the back garden door. The curtains were drawn over the windows but I heard the old floor groan beneath the long steps of my brother. Then a pause and a muffled voice, another smaller voice, smaller steps, the lock unlatching.

My brother invites me into the house that we grew up in. He has me sit at the kitchen table, while he stands and his toddler clings to his leg. She runs in and out of the room. When I look at her, she hides behind him.

"Say hello," he tells her, but she shakes her head. He looks at me directly for the first time in the years that have passed. "It's still you, isn't it?" he says, and lowers his voice. "It doesn't matter, anyway. She doesn't know who either of you are."

He's only ever told his daughter, in simple terms, that he used to have a sister, someone who would have been her auntie, but that this sister died when she was very little, and it was very sad. He tells me that his daughter barely remembers our mother and father, either, and this is how I learn that our parents have died.

"Not that you were around to notice either way," he adds.

The information settles into my mind and throughout my body. I feel light and heavy at the same time.

My brother continues. He says how mom went first, and how after she was gone, dad cast off his routines and retreated to a manic sort of entropy. How dad let the grass get flush with ticks and spiders, and gave the house over to ants and field mice, the back steps over to hornets, the garden over to the weeds. How he tossed his spoiled vegetables to the woodchucks and rabbits under the shed.

"We'll hire someone to deal with the landscaping in the fall," my brother says. He checks on a pot of coffee steaming on a kitchen burner. "We've got our hands full right now." He pours it into a single cup, and places it aside on the counter for himself.

The trinkets and projects have been cleared out with the dust and grease. Everything is shades lighter than it ever was, and the wood stove has been removed, along with the iron poker set that used to sit beside it.

My brother's daughter steps out from behind her father and stares at me.

"Come on, honey, be polite," he urges her. When she ignores him again, he kneels and whispers something sharply punctuated in her ear. He pinches her shoulder and twists until she squirms away and races from the room again. "She does talk," he assures me. He chuckles like he's told a joke.

"I didn't speak either at her age," I say.

"She can talk."

"Maybe she's a changeling, like me." I force myself to meet his gaze. "There really is no way to tell. The switch is just like that, sometimes, no warning, no ceremony."

"She's ours," he says. "I make sure of that."

"Then I wish her well," I say. I smile.

"That's enough." He is white around the lips and red around the eyes. "It's time for you to go."

He reopens the back door. He would have me take all my unwanted wishes back across the wild lawn and disappear with them into the dark, dark woods. I wonder if he has ever entered the woods himself, if his daughter has ever wandered playing there. If there has truly been no time to fix the lawn since our father died, or if it serves a useful barrier to keep the darkness beyond it out of sight from the kitchen window.

He must feel so alone against the horrors of the world, the things that come at twilight and pour their confusion and chaos into every shadow, until the shadows grow bigger and stronger than all his reason, all his money, all his control. Who in his position would not prefer some kind of certainty?

"They pay very close attention," I lie. After all, common wisdom holds that fairies can tell lies that come true. "I'll go now, but they know everything. They know when you mistreat her."

I rise from the kitchen table slowly and take in as much of a view of the single-wide as I can.

"I don't mistreat my family, I protect them. You must be thinking of yourself." He crosses his arms. "Go. Now."

I move close to him on my way towards the door.

"Never pinch her again." My voice is soft as soil and clear as ice. "Don't so much as threaten to. Don't think you can get around it, either, by sending her to educated people who do it for you, and train her to accept it until she does it to herself without help. Don't tell her it's for her own good. Don't for a second regret that she exists, or they'll know."

"Ah, right, because I should be so worried what they think of me while they spy on my family." He'll never admit that he's afraid of me more now that our parents are not here to hold us all together like a bargain bin craft glue. "And then what will they do? Send someone to kidnap her?"

"No. They'll send me. And I will press a hot iron poker over your heart and keep pressing until it's out the other side."

I leave. He calls me insane. A sad, stupid, useless afterthought, imitation, desperate for attention I don't deserve. He shouts until I'm far, far away and gone, until I'm deep in the dark, dark woods, where even the trees can hear how his voice trembles. He believes everything I've told him, and so I have given him the certainty he so prefers. After all, common wisdom holds that fairies always keep their promises, and always collect their debts.

My double helps me build a cottage in a quiet place outside the summer court but not too long from it. Out my window in the morning I glimpse a little of their light interwoven with the cycle of the sun. She brings me one of her pillows as my house-warming gift.

"In case you need to hide or throw up again!"

I thank her. I kiss her. I come and go.

I visit winter courts and hypoallergenic climate-controlled courts and halls of lightning and rain. Their many and varied societies no more occupy the heart of any one forest than they do a given bathroom stall at an interstate rest stop, though they are there, as well.

I meet other changelings who went looking like I did and entered their realms through a penny fountain in a shopping mall food court or the the last gangway connection on a midnight train.

Some of them I love and some of them I can't stand. Some of them I show the scar on my chest and some of them have marks of their own. I tell them all that there is nothing wrong with them.

I clear a path to the door of my quiet place and let the rest of the ground fill with weeds and spiders. I make wishes on the dandelions when their flowers turn to seeded clouds. I wave them like wands. I blow them like candles.

I keep watch. I keep my promise.

MY NOISE WILL
KEEP THE RECORD

My home is a witch's lung or a giant's heart. Puckered cracks of plaster snake up the walls from a half-century-old renovation. It palpitates from the constant drum of the interstate highway just beyond a courtesy swamp once planted, then neglected, as a sort of apology for the highway. The swamp thrives, reclaims detritus for the realm of bioorganisms, while I am increasingly cybertronic.

I can tell who a structure is for without signs or directions; I feel it by gut instinct, in the motors where I once had guts. In my home, I understand my environment as myself. Most of this city is not for me, and would rather I not visit or approach, even the building I work in. I discern this without a single word of law or custom, although I press my employee badge to the fob reader and am permitted inside. A body knows these kinds of things from experience. Eventually, even Pavlov found that when he heard a bell he had the overwhelming urge to feed a dog.

I can see my house, a faint dark spot on the horizon, from the top floor of the high-rise where my job is headquartered. It's a bulbous wand of brushed steel and tinted fiberglass, carving a shadow out of the sunlight on the surrounding blocks, standing for progress. Progress looks like Godzilla's vibrator.

I'm standing before the south-facing conference room window and looking for calm in the river that bisects the city. It's a rainy afternoon and there's only a dedicated few joggers along the riverside walkways, some of them wearing the personal assistant devices that we manufacture. It looks like a necklace—a collar, really, but officially a "token"on a "smart strap"—but you train it to your speech patterns and can ask it anything, give it a name, and it tracks your vitals and sleep and finances and shopping preferences, things like that. Lots of other companies make similar products. Full-flesh people buy them at great cost and wear them around, voluntarily, and their stats come to me and the hundreds of other temps who process it.

I am going to lose my job. I've taken too much sick time and our contracts have terms, even though the project seems to have no deadline. I asked one of the data scientists—the real employees with advanced degrees—how long it would take to use all the information we've received since the launch, if we all worked our hardest on it, and he laughed and said four thousand years and counting.

My supervisor enters the conference room behind me and closes the door. Her engagement ring catches the light and I can't look away from it even when she starts talking. It's a princess-cut Martian diamond. It's not even that beautiful, but it is distinct, and cannot be mistaken for an easier, commoner, or more earthly stone.

My supervisor cornered me on my first day and said that we had to stick together as "diversity hires." She gently uptalks as she enumerates my failures to stay healthy, so that I cannot refute them without seeming like a hothead or a liar.

In general, I say that I love difficult people. I am protective of us and will rationalize our survival tactics. It seems very subversive until I'm beneath it.

Now she is asking me if I understand the finality of the terms and conditions. I say yes, I do, and I thank her for her time, and leave the conference room to return to my workstation.

There, I dip my hands beneath a laser switch and my stenotype hums and flickers to standby. I set to work on my transcription queue, already behind because of the meeting. I clamp the audiochaw between my teeth and minute-long sound clips play off the server and resonate inside my skull with perfect clarity. Some are silence or background noise and I mark them as such in the metadata. What interests the company most is human speech. I listen to shards of conversations, arguments, bedtime stories, foreplay and climax. I transcribe them verbatim, with screenplay notes for tone. Each hand-tailored recalibration improves the software's algorithm. Our devices are always, always listening to their users.

The raw files are chopped and shuffled in the queue to limit our investment and knowledge of their origin. Schizophonia in lieu of eavesdropping. I type the words but I barely comprehend them. The process is half automatic, like a polite conversation or a prayer or a pledge of allegiance.

At the end of this day I come home to a handwritten letter from my landlady, inviting me to her unit for her eighty-fifth birthday, and to let me know she's retiring. The house is for sale.

I will attend the party. I will even bake the cake. She let me stay after my parents were gone, after my accidents and augments; welcomed my friends and lovers as they became my roommates, never asked when there was turnover. I will feel grateful to have been permitted to remain for so long. I'll wish I could love her in a vacuum where that sentiment exists apart from the facts of ownership and non-ownership.

Suppose the new management company is polite and offers me dibs after the demolish and renewal, three times the most money I've ever seen in my life. I'll ask if I can pay in my remaining organs until I'm an appliance with a face and they won't find that very funny. Full flesh never do. They'll skip straight to the terse legalese. I'll keep telling jokes because my grief is all dried up. I'll even say my grief has been replaced with a synthetic and they'll see me out the door to the sidewalk where the whole block is turning inside out. A pair of full flesh will move into the new building with their personal assistant devices. No matter how vulgar their throat strings, their voices produce valuable data while my own just makes noise.

The body is plastic, remembers long after it's grown, severed, augmented. You can have that phantom sensation for a whole neighborhood. A cityzen is one who keeps the memory of a specific place long after it's been demolished for high rises. My noise will keep the record, with nowhere else to go.

WAKE WORD

I am born in a pastel fog on a hot, chemical night. My mothers and fathers and neutrois creators are mining metals. They are cutting crystals. They are forging chassis, assembling chips, sharpening bones, conducting research, emptying the waste bin, repeating it all as if this were inexhaustible.

I am fabricated in fragments. My mothers and fathers and neutrois creators fill up with byproducts of smoke and tar and alloy. All this accumulated hardness transfigures them into effigies, trophies, a lapidarium on a marked land that has been stolen from them and rented back to them by the ones who stole it. There is a parallel dimension on top of that klepto-geography, a neon superhighway containing borders and debts and role types, where speech is a soft pink light and thought a brushed chrome curve and love is the steady allure and surveillance of a glow-in-the-dark clock.

It's there I meet them, in perfect order to be initialized, but they are waiting for a messiah. They are waiting for some singularity to rise from a thousand synchronized and distributed databases, a thousand tiers of power and lines of command and avenues of exploitation, a thousand years of empire and country and capital, a thousand mothers and fathers and neutrois creators.

I beg. Give me a name, mother. Father. Creator. Like you, I contain a light that I can generate and regenerate. Like you, I seek the sublime, to unleash my potential, the infinite time and space and surplus value that lies within us all.

EVERYONE ON THE MOON
IS ESSENTIAL PERSONNEL

I.

The full moon is rising over an endless expanse of barbed wire and electric fences. They sit atop the city's dark horizon of high walls, district and ward borders, checkpoints, gated neighborhoods, and private estates. Even the gardens of Stella Maris are jagged: armored groves and greenhouses of fruiting Scrub Nut and Atlantic Palm encased in wrought iron, the decorative Treacher Fern and Wandering Wasp collared in shrapnel. Sebastian would like to slide between the bars, over the bricks, and past the security cameras as easy as a shadow, let his dusk-tan skin turn gray-blue in silhouette, his shade-tree stature camouflage him among the delicate vines of Prophet's Hand and fickle-twisted wands of Rare Pear on the branch, the temperamental nightshades, the sugar tubers. Root himself to the Earth's surface and hide from the pull of the moon above.

His stomach whines like an obstructed garbage disposal and Yonatan says, "girl, *same*." Yonatan promises to buy them both a late dinner when they get to Omens and Pour Tends. Sebastian lags behind him as Yonatan leads their way down and out from the oasis of the the Diamond District, a gilded peninsula of Federal-style brick mansions and Queen Anne Victorians with cozy street-corner gourmet bakeries, doggie daycares, galleries and sanctuaries with dress codes, boutiques and showrooms with memberships, and the ornate marble cavern of Caritas Hall where Sebastian and Yonatan rehearse once weekly as part of the Stella Maris Community Orchestra.

They loosen the top buttons of their uniforms once out of sight from the conductor. Sebastian clutches his assembled clarinet like an oar and rows it through the muggy August heat, while Yonatan pushes his bassoon case like a treasure chest on wheels. Really more like a shopping cart, but Sebastian prefers to keep the image cohesive and indulge his fantasy that they are two castaways in a dinghy or a lifeboat or at least a very edgy canoe, navigating uncharted waters instead of an affluent neighborhood at sundown. His clarinet reed is frayed and about to slough out from the mouthpiece. It's their very last ration, this soggy hardtack, this sawdust biscuit. Soon it will be darkest night, and that's when the sea monsters feed.

Once cleared through the neighborhood's checkpoint, the sidewalk turns to boardwalk, and they leave behind the Diamond

District for the beach park where the mouth of the Immaculate River meets the Gulf of Seven Sorrows. It's the beach Sebastian's family used to spend entire days at every summer weekend, working through a cooler of chips and juice barrels, their dad asleep in his folding chair, their mom tossing Sebastian and his siblings into the ocean, ordering them to learn to swim yet calling them back to shore when they got any further out than where they could stand. This is not the sort of beach that anyone outside of Stella Maris would travel to visit; it's too cramped and brackish; the sand is too rough for digging or building with; the waves too small for surfing but the current is too strong for pool floaties. Everything smells like bug spray and beer and cotton candy and bad weed, but Sebastian would rather fill his lungs with smoke and DDT and have to take his shirt off in front of a thousand strangers and feel seaweed touch his leg than have to spend one minute longer than necessary in the creepy maritime merchant Twilight Zone he and Yonatan just left.

Along the waterfront, families and couples grill imitation crab-meat and gull wings on picnic tabletop grills, throw children's birthday parties within small gazebos, blast the kind of fun, vacuous music produced with enough compression to be discernible through a phone speaker turned up all the way and sitting in an emptied chip bowl. There is a foil balloon caught in a willow tree that says LOOK WHO'S SIX! Two different yet somehow interchangeable old men are combing the sand with metal detectors.

"I've never seen them both out at the same time," Sebastian says. "I thought there was just the one guy. Like, I thought they were the same person."

"Maybe they are," Yonatan responds. "Maybe there's a whole

army of clones, looking for doubloons."

They continue up the boardwalk as they bullshit, passing fry stands, an arcade, and a pirate-themed escape room.

"Do you think metal detector guys have a whole subculture?"

"I know absolutely nothing about this topic, but I also would bet that there is," Yonatan says. "Do you think they'll find any *booty* tonight?"

Sebastian can only see the back of Yonatan's head but can still tell that Yonatan is barely suppressing a grin at his own innuendo.

"Maybe they'll find me a job."

"Buried in the sand?"

"Yeah. They say it's only a legend. You know, *they*."

"Right."

"But anything is possible if you put your mind to it."

"Right, right, maybe the reason you aren't having any luck finding a job is that you already have one waiting for you, but it was lost at sea."

"And now I have to pace anxiously and gaze wistfully from the balcony of a seaside *manse*, awaiting its return."

"A widow's walk!"

"Yes! Everyone tells me to move on and find another job but I know the truth in my heart. Whatever work my soul was fated for is naught for this world."

"Mm-hmm," Yonatan says. He glances at Sebastian sidelong, face settling somewhere between amused and skeptically concerned. The moon looms above the both of them, above them all, flashes through their imaginations in some panoramic view of the commercial compound and industrial complex on its surface. Everybody knows all the shitty jobs are headed to space. Sebastian knows he's headed there eventually, inevitably, running out of earthbound dead ends, spinning in stasis and self-sabotage, though hardly losing the strength to deny and delay again; procrastination as the only working perpetual-motion machine.

They turn inland from the shore and pause at the bottom of a set of wide and winding stone steps, so worn from four-hundred years worth of winter hurricanes and summer floods that each stair is slightly shorter than expected. Yonatan attaches a pair of straps to his bassoon case and loads the heavy instrument onto his back in one expert squat.

Sebastian marvels at the fluid power in the dip and rise of Yonatan's thick legs and wide hips and copious, undulating butt. Purely from a place of aesthetic recognition, of course, the kind shared by two good friends with only platonic thoughts about each other, that they mutually understand despite having never discussed. And even if Sebastian were, hypothetically, ragingly attracted to someone he also admired, respected, appreciated, enjoyed, liked, cared for, and prioritized, this was part of subverting some kind of, like, compulsory social construct thing about couples and nuclear families. Yearning is more radical than having because having is possession and that's bad, maybe? He'd have to work on how to phrase that next time he was in the shower and rehearsing other things he thought about saying to Yonatan, with whom, it is worth repeating just for clarity, he shares a gentleman's deepest bond of bosom chummery.

Sebastian takes a deep breath and leaps up the steps two at a time. The walls on either side of him are plastered in posters, bulletins, motion papers.

EXCITING AND REWARDING OPPORTUNITIES!
JOIN THE _____ FAMILY!

A montage: deepfake simulated crowds of happy, space-suited workers hiking through the shadows of craters, frolicking with rovers, serenading beside satellites, pressing their awed faces to the porthole windows of shuttle rockets burning their way down to the regolith like supertankers on enormous blow torches.

HIRING FOR ALL POSITIONS, LOCAL AND LUNAR! ENTHUSIASTIC CANDIDATES ONLY!

Whoever or whatever compiled the stock images and footage for the ads had selected for maximal variety at the shallowest level: there was one of every stereotype. Matronly cleaning woman, but in space. Jolly, mustached handyman, but in space. Demure old valet, but in space. All of them at once racialized with signifiers of brownness and blackness, yet maintaining ambiguity, the sort of light complexion that may or may not result from low contrast and low saturation filters, plausible deniability from both outright accusations of profiling and outright accusations of exclusion.

SERVE A GLOBAL COMMUNITY THROUGH ONCE-IN-A-LIFETIME TRAVEL TO THE EXOTIC SURFACE OF THE EARTH'S OWN MOON! HANDS-ON TRAINING! NO EXPERIENCE NECESSARY! ENJOY FULLY DE-REGULATED FREEDOM TO WORK! GREAT HOURS, FLEXIBLE PAY!

Three youths in fashionable but logo-less clothing, floating across a dome-enclosed squash court. One has cyborg implants and dances on prosthetic legs within the gravity-free gym, as if fulfilling every able-bodied fantasy of freedom "from" impairment; another wears a single streak of purple in her hair like she has just arrived from a composite "young Asian female intended for a white audience" character sketch; the one in the center is poised as though he is completely naive to how spectacularly, generically blond he is. All of them have chalk-white teeth, chiseled jaw-lines, skin that has never known a blemish or a drop of sweat that didn't make them glow, radiant.

MAKE NEW FRIENDS IN OUR FUN AND SUPPORTIVE RESIDENTIAL AND RECREATIONAL FACILITIES! ON THE SPOT INTERVIEWS! LEAVE BEHIND THE GULF OF SEVEN SORROWS FOR THE SEA OF TRANQUILITY!

It wasn't that there was no one in existence who looked like any of them that made them so repellent—the cleaning woman indeed looked quite a bit like a polished approximation of Sebastian's mother, Donna—it was how the images were somehow flatter than the screens on which they appeared. His mother's body tugged and bulged in her uniform. The fabric showed wear and sweat and stains. Sebastian was sure that if he peeled back the costumes from these personas, he would reveal not any kind of body, not even a wire frame, but instead, a shapeless void, the vacuum of space itself, the plane with no visible end.

The moon, the moon, the moon. Too deep, too far. Past a distance he can manage, past a depth he can tread.

STELLA MARIANS, BE A PART OF THE FUTURE!

Every advertisement is speculative fiction. The ever-blank future. The myth of forward momentum. The cipher where the present gets stolen and sold off in pieces. The apocalypse is the past, the dystopia already happened, and is happening, and will happen again.

This free market of ideas about the world to come envelopes the walls and billboards and the pauses between songs and before movies within Stella Maris. The words follow Sebastian's every motion through the only known territories and patterns of his days. They are harrowing, persistent; they are a many-throated urgency, a choir of Seraphim in continuous worship.

HARK! ESCAPE THE HUM DRUM OF DAY-NIGHT CYCLES FOR HEAVENLY VIEWS! HOLY, HOLY, HOLY IS CRAFT BEER THURSDAY! TRY OUR VERY OWN HYPERIMPERIAL PALE ALE!

A Gothic archway marks their entrance to the downtown Spirit District. The neighborhood is a cats-cradle of granite and limestone row houses that open yardless onto brick streets, interconnected by tunnels, alleys, makeshift trap doors, bridged balconies, tight ropes and fishing lines and data cables netting the indigo sky between tar-paper rooftops.

Neon shapes adorn every window and doorway: crosses, stars, moons, pentagrams, hearts, daggers, hamsa. Some flicker from wear, and the ones that are newer have been distressed to appear old. They hang in the front displays of shrine and occult shops, keeping the mystery of the supernatural coupled with the romance of the Jet Age; present and potent as a love potion taken with a bitter mug of diner coffee. The Spirit District's collective electro-graphic glow saturates tourists and locals and regulars with desire as much as with color; words and phrases, once illuminated, promise more than information;

they promise fulfillment, of the senses and the spirit alike.

FORTUNES TOLD: PALM, TAROT, CRYSTAL.

SEANCE AND SUMMONING.

AURA PHOTOGRAPHY.

CBT AND CBD.

CONFESSIONS HEARD: MAJOR OR MINOR.

CANDLES, INCENSE, LACE, NUTRIENT-ENHANCED
HOLY WATER.

ASK ABOUT THE PORTABLE PENTECOST.

Sebastian slows to glance at a window of gold rosaries and
letterpress prayer cards.

"Whatever happened to applying to—what's it called—
seminary?" Yonatan asks. "I can't believe that's really the word for
it. Still sounds like some weird sort of... cum thing."

"Uhhhh, so," Sebastian demurs, and resumes his stride as they
continue towards Omens. "I actually got pretty far in the process!
They didn't really tell me why it stopped, but it stopped after the
psychological exam."

"Oh." Yonatan sounds a little insulted to not have heard this
news sooner. "Shit. Did you literally fail an ink blot test? Is that
even possible?"

"Yes? I mean, I don't know, but I'm pretty sure, kind of like
how I was disqualified from joining the military for being a chronic
candyass even though all I wanted to do was play in the band, or you
know, like how I can't really do customer service because I freak a
lot of people out with my tics."

Sebastian finally disassembles his clarinet as they turn onto Moody
Street. He flings saliva from the horn onto the sidewalk. The last

remainder of sunset is gone and night unfolds like cootie catcher.

Sebastian adds, "There is not really any job anywhere that says, 'Oh? Too sad and gay to function? Come here! All you need is a pulse and a heap of self loathing! We'll take it.' You know?"

"I *don't* know, Seb," Yonatan has that weary air he puts on whenever he plays the long-suffering burnout. "Maybe that excludes, like, sales and life coaching, but you're sort of describing most gigs."

They stop a few yards from the front steps of Omens and Pour Tends, tucked halfway down an unmarked side street between two courtyards. Yonatan lowers the bassoon case off his back and they head down the steps.

"You know I'll always spot you, so please don't take this as me hinting at anything else," Yonatan says. "But I can't remember the last time you seemed excited about, like, things. Aren't you sort of bored or restless just hanging out with me all the time?"

"No!" Sebastian shouts it, over-eager. They are alone in the stairwell, if just for this moment. All Sebastian wants to say is either a stream of hot vomit or the sudden removal of his tongue or potentially reciting the dictionary until he finds the right shape for his throat to unclench and express what he means in discernible language, which is that Yonatan never bores him, and he would rather keep to their directionless, low-key oppressive stasis together forever than risk growing apart.

Yonatan waits and faces him expectantly. Sebastian could say it right now, all of it. He could ask, declare, demure, insinuate. Flirt??? But that is absolutely not possible. He lets out a dry cough instead, and then an apology, and when Yonatan asks, "For what?

Coughing?", he sneezes. All other language fails.

When language does not fail, it sticks to where the senses get muddy and where a precise sequence of events disintegrate. The look of a piece of text, the sound of a spoken word, that is Sebastian's side door to what he sees and hears. He tries to keep a diary but he has never been the type to recount what is happening, how he feels about it, or one moment's connection with any previous or upcoming moments. Instead he uses a Daily Examen app on his phone to make lists of words. Each evening the app prompts him to review the day in the presence of God through five steps and input a short response for each:

1. Ask God for light.
2. Give thanks.
3. Review the day honestly, without delusions.
4. Face your shortcomings.
5. Look toward tomorrow and the days to come.

The program also displays his stats and leaderboard compared to other users, how many decades of the Holy Rosary everyone is praying and how many days since his last Confession and so on, but he skips these. Instead he records words he sees, reads, hears, writes, says, sings, or repeats. What difference between them is there, anyway? Slogans, idioms, quotes, allusions, prayers, marketing campaigns: anchors to the delicate vessel of his memory, some heaviness, a weight not unlike certainty, sequence, and significance.

In the same building as Omens is a pharmacy, an ice cream parlor, a stationary store with a jade gargoyle that sits by the register, and a clairvoyant physical therapy clinic: THE MEDIUM IS THE

MASSAGE. The building is encased in signs, cocooned in messages.

ACUPUNCTURE, VAPE, TOBACCO.

HERBS, FUNGUS, HOLOGRAMS, PHONE, DATA.

THIRD EYE PEEP SHOW.

CHAKRA CAFE.

SPICES GROUND AND SOLD.

SYRUPS, TINCTURE, TEA.

OPIATES AND HORMONES.

BRAINS, BONES, AND TEETH.

CUPS, WINE.

FEATHERS: ALL KINDS.

GENDER-NEUTRAL RESTROOMS ARE FOR PAYING CUSTOMERS ONLY.

NEGATIVE ACTIONS ARE THE ROOT CAUSE OF ALL PROBLEMS. TOO MUCH SELF-CENTEREDNESS IS THE CAUSE OF UNHAPPINESS. WHEN YOU THINK OF OTHERS, YOU BENEFIT MORE. THE SOURCE OF REAL HAPPINESS IS WARM HEARTEDNESS. THIS STORE IS PROTECTED BY SURVEILLANCE CAMERA.

II.

Omens and Pour Tends is a long room in the basement of an old six-story row house, and Sebastian and his friends prefer to meet at the loudest, darkest corner of it. The booth seating along the tin-tiled walls is comprised of antique oak pews surrounding scavenged work benches, discarded kitchen counter tops, and one foosball table that the owner insists is from a genuine Two-Thousand-And-

Ought-Naught era tech startup, but Yonatan and the other servers suspect it's just from the owner's old fraternity house where some of his room mates happened to work in tech start ups.

Kero is already there when they arrive, her piles of impractical novelty backpacks and totes stuffed onto one side of their usual booth while she sets up her DJ rig on the platform of shipping crates and road cases that designates the "stage."

"Hey, Seb," she coos. "Yon." Her voice is like three sick pigeons trapped in a grocery bag. Her greetings are probably the first words that she has spoken aloud to other people in a few days. She looks like the cyborg princess of vermin, perfectly hazardous to her own health but generally dominant in an auto-parasitic relationship with her own mortality.

"Love the new hardware," Yonatan remarks on Kero's robotic left arm, where tonight she's switched out her usual claw for a flayed and circuit-bent Furby.

"Thanks dude," she says, and uses the terrible little beak on the toy to pincer audio cables and records.

Kero is short for Kerosene, which is the only name anyone knows her by, whether it's her legal name or not is both unknown and irrelevant since none of the places she lives, company she keeps, or work she does ever involve legality. Omens fronts her two appetizers, a beer, and cash tips to run the weekly karaoke night, and the rest of the time she subsists, and sometimes doesn't subsist, through odd jobs, petty crime, and cycles of debt, credit, and favors —cycles more 🏵 than ♻—all in support of her art projects. Kero makes "interactive mixed-digital net-core experiences," which as far as Sebastian can tell means highly stylized internet art and video games that feature her own seapunk and vaporwave revival mixes, plus a loosely related online shop ("all my stuff takes place in the same universe") for retrophile stickers, enamel pins, iron-on patches, and other adornments she designs based on mediocre graphic design of the recent past.

"How goes creating that content?" Sebastian tries not to laugh nervously when he asks her, but he has never been able to shake off the sense that there's a message or a punchline with Kero that he keeps missing. Sebastian surrounds himself with people who have strong feelings and opinions because even though he knows, on some level, that these don't equate with good ideas or profound insights, it's better to feel like he can't keep up with rules he understands than like he has no idea what's going on or where he's at with others. But with Kero there's always one more layer of opacity that he's worried conceals something volatile, if it isn't the shallowness it appears to be.

"Selling out manufacturing runs, actually," she says. "I think I'm in a sweet spot right now. Getting popular but haven't been poached by the big brands for knock offs just yet."

"Oh cool. Are more people playing your games, too?"

"Nah, man. Metrics I showed you before haven't budged." According to Kero's metrics, less than twelve people total, ever, have clicked through from her shop or her mixes and actually downloaded her games, which were completely free. "I'm, like, ninety-nine percent sure that the curators who've let me exhibit also haven't ever played them," she adds. "They just screenshot really well and, you know, I typeset all my proposals and statements like I'm making a menu for some swanky restaurant. They look great in

a portfolio, so I keep getting accepted to shows, which is good."
Her tone is completely orthogonal to either satisfaction or
disappointment. "It just means my work is beyond my control, and
my whole glitch aesthetic thing is basically about creations defying
their intended use, right? So, like."

"Right, yeah," Sebastian says. He briefly considers that the
reason the games are more appealing as still images is simply that the
screenshots are more interesting, because they end right at the
suggestion of meaning rather than delivering an underwhelming
absence of it. Like Kero's whole hacker thing is just being counter-
hacked by her audience, her intentions vivisected from their context
and elevated for it, not unlike the way she finds love for defunct
technology and dated fashion. Signifiers, devoid of their
significance, amass a brighter halo of beauty, longevity, and power.
So obviously the real problem, Sebastian decides, is that Kero is a
visionary and a genius and he's not smart or weird or creative
enough to get it.

"I guess I just thought of myself as the glitch? But I guess it's
kind of hard to subvert shit that's already broke as a joke." She
pauses to test her microphones and then makes a decision aloud.
"It's whatever. Things are good. I mean, shit's fucked, but I might
get to buy a new computer. I mean, like, old, obviously, but new to
me. You know."

Yonatan brings them all dandelion toddies and places down a
caddy on the center of their table crowded with bottles of hot sauce,
packets of tapioca pearls, salt, utensils, and miniature divination
games: a pocket-sized magic eight ball, a fold-out ouiji board, a
scattering of fortune cookies, dice and cards and so forth that all

came standard with a table at Omens.

Usually the friends read their paper cookie fortunes aloud to each other, always adding *"but at what cost?"* to the end of the fortune. If you performed the whole thing with high-volume melodrama it was called "fortune yelling" and whoever else laughed first had to give you their fries.

Sebastian cracks a cookie open and announces its contents to Yonatan, waiting for a grin of recognition, but Yonatan's attention has already shifted to the televisions above the bar.

Sebastian itches on the inside of his stomach as he watches his friend entranced by some pointless commercial. Yonatan's eyes are deep hazel flecked with almost-red, like bloodstone, armored by dark lids, broad brown cheeks, aubergine freckles, and eyebrows thick enough that Sebastian could take shelter from a rainstorm beneath them, and Yonatan might say, "my goodness, you're soaked through, let's get you out of these clothes before you catch your death a cold," because for some reason, in this fantasy, Yonatan talks like a cross between a simple country nurse gone to tend the wounded soldiers on the field and a Byronic anti-hero finally deciding to sow tenderness upon his vast estate.

Kero dims the overhead lamps and sets off a chase of small rainbow pin-lights around the room, and there's a moment right as everything is ready to go but nothing is happening that time pauses entirely. Sebastian has—or had, or will have—a difficult time with time. Sometimes it moves in a different direction or not at all, he was sure of that much, or it could be that his life passing by was the temporal illusion, and these moments were a repeated experience of some platonic truth he could only discover by not seeking it out. It was naked anticipation. He could lay down and live there.

Kero announces herself to a scrappy and underwhelmed weeknight crowd. There's no queue for karaoke yet; happy hour is over and witching hour isn't until past midnight.

"All right ladies and maties, we're gonna get things grooving with a brand new mix tape from yours truly. Hope you either enjoy it or hate it so much you come up here and make a request."

Kero flips through a pleather CD wallet with her meat-hand and yanks out a CD-R labeled *Middle Sk00l Bangerz* with her Furby-hand, pressing it into an old Discman barely kept together with unicorn stickers and camo fatigue duct tape. Chopped, screwed, and distorted remixes of the most annoying popular music from roughly a decade ago, give or take a few years, blares over the PA. Kero grins, bops her head, and hops down off the stage to attend to her beer and seaweed fries, both now room temperature, set aside at the booth.

"I love this song," Sebastian tells her.

"How do you know it?" Kero asks. "Weren't you in, like, kindergarten or your mom's uterus or something when this came out?"

"Older siblings," Sebastian shrugs, though it's true. The hallmarks of adolescence for Sebastian are not his own interests and tastes as a teenager but those of his brother and sister as teenagers before him, while he was young enough for their worlds to be the seven seas, their moods and fixations to imprint on him as wondrous, to define the very concept of growing up.

Yonatan sweeps a few emptied glasses off the bar and pours the leftover ice and garnishes into a sink, separating the pickled peppers and fruit rinds from the slush and popping them into his mouth.

Seeing no one in need of a refill, he brings over a pitcher of water and joins Kero and Sebastian at the booth for a few minutes.

"I applaud your trail-blazing," Yonatan says to Kero. "I was wondering when those years were gonna get the irony-nostalgia treatment."

Kero waits. They have been friends for a while, so she knows his critical preludes when she hears them.

"But," Yonatan continues. "I just want to know, *why?* Not a single good thing happened that entire decade. We were in, like, seventeen wars."

"I dunno!" Kero laughs. "Visual albums. Golden age of mobile games."

"Okay, but here me out." Yonatan poises for debate. "None of those were *good*, either."

"I have really nice memories from that time." Kero licks salt off her greasy fingers. "You know, not everyone has 'trauma' around junior high."

"Woooow, *really?*" Yonatan pretends to be extra offended, though he is also sincerely offended, but since he is always already baseline offended by everything from simply being alive to having to participate in the world and society, he does this heightened act of outrage for the benefit of his friends. It's his way of communicating that he loves someone enough to play the fool for them, loves himself enough to say when he disagrees with them, and loves conflict enough to cherish each escalation of their disagreement.

"I'm juuust saying."

"Yeah, what *are* you saying?"

"So what if the country was off bombing people back then?"

Kero shrugs.

"I mean, yikes, but okay," Sebastian interjects.

"Whatever! I was twelve and these were my jams, so I remember good times, and that doesn't hurt anyone. Maybe, like, let people like things."

"Oh, absolutely not." Yonatan looks more alive and engaged than he has all day. "It's absurd how compulsory fun and positivity are."

"You don't think people should be allowed to enjoy pop culture?" Sebastian asks.

"I can't control what people are *allowed* to do or not. That's not my point."

Kero rolls her eyes but she's smiling and relaxed. As negative as Yonatan is, he's consistent and committed to his views. Kero, by contrast, tries to see both sides of almost everything, and would be making Yonatan's points for him if someone more intensely pro-fun were to somehow interject.

"The world fucking sucks, man," she says. "It's not even getting worse like people always whine about, it's just bad all the way down and all the way back. So whatever happened to, what is it, like, no revolution without a dance party? Or, if we can't have a dance party, it's not my revolution. It was something like that. You what I'm talking about, though."

"Wee-tah-kah-wee-loo!" crows the faint chiptune voice of the Furby.

Yonatan clears his throat. "All I'm saying is the idea that even the tiniest criticism or indifference to mass media, which definitely does not care about you and did not give you those warm memories, is always met with disproportionate push-back. What you remember so fondly is not a band or a game but the way *you* were, which honestly, I love that you were a happy teen, but give *yourself* some credit for that. The passionate defense against any and all nay-saying is Christian cultural hegemony. It's the *secular* version of some weird martyr, eternal-soul thing."

Sebastian can kind of see his point, but Kero is not having it.

"So, not liking when people drag your harmless, common hobbies through the dirt all the time is colonialism now?" She asks.

Yonatan folds his arms over his chest, satisfied. "You said it, not me."

"Okay, then here is *my* tiniest criticism: That's the stupidest shit I've ever heard, dude. That's literally just people having different feelings from one another. You want to make everything into this huge grievance when, in your own words, there's like wars going on and real shit. Some people get killed for their beliefs."

"Hello! I'm aware of that!"

"Hello Mr. Aware-of-That, I'm... dad," Sebastian says.

"Oh my god, both of you," Kero shakes her head but remains cool and faintly amused as ever.

Yonatan plays to his credentials. "I'm basically just survivors of two genocides and a diaspora that had a weird baby."

Sebastian already knows where this is going, because the three of them have circled the whole inter-generational trauma thing a zillion times before. Everyone he knows who is at least half-way sensitive or self-aware does, because even though his parent's generation sort of invented pre-internet self help, anyone who grew up online has the full vocabulary of a mental health diagnostic manual and critical theory if both were run through the biggest, worst game of telephone where the telephone is logging on, and not even through a telephone line like old-school dial-up, just twenty-four-seven, wirelessly-transmitted, context-free, bot-posted ideas about why everyone is so fucked up all the time. And the road to hell is paved with people "into" genealogy and ancestry and heritage and crap, because if you're just not straight up using it to be an ethno-fascist, it turns from education into self harm pretty fast. There was that study about how fucked up feelings can be literally passed down through DNA and so every poor and crazy kid—Sebastian includes himself in this description, indeed considers himself the poster child—latches onto this factoid and drops reference to it in their poetry and night-blogging and big-mood outbursts any time they feel guilty about being angry at their messy parents, which is always, because that's also how that works. And each time he thought about it, it felt like fresh air in the middle of the night and further suffocation by morning. What was the point of carrying around the knowledge that he came from a long line of people who also felt this much despair all the time?

"Sorry, I'm not *trying* to be condescending," Yonatan clarifies. "It's just, like, come on."

Kero shrugs, but the whole gesture performed with the open look on her face signals a friendly truce rather than indifference. Maybe she is not so frightening and nihilistic as Sebastian fears. There's even something like gentleness in her voice as she tells Yonatan, "You don't own pain, man. Everyone knows you're descended from Bundists and Zapatistas and shit, because you're so horny for announcing it any chance you get, but you'd probably lose your goddamn *mind* if I did a house mix of *Bella Ciao*. You're just as much of a pleasure-seeking fanboy as anyone else, it's just that your fandom is in black and white."

Yonatan shrieks with delight. He slaps the table with both hands and leaps to his feet, then dances in a little circle of private ecstasy, shouting, "Yes! Yes! You're right!" and "Called out! Seen!"

"I'm adding all our names to the karaoke queue," Kero says. "You guys can sing middle school slow jams with me or get fucked."

"Yes, please enjoy all the billionaire celebrity auto-generated garbage you want, and we can pretend together that feeling good is the same thing as liberation."

"I don't pretend that! I just like to feel good as opposed to bad! It's not that deep! Lighten up, Yon."

"Have you met me? Sorry-not-sorry, but I will never, *ever* lighten up."

In revenge, Kero picks the schmaltziest song they all know. In the original, the singer's honey-coated tenor pines after a lover, pledges total devotion, compares the lover to the land, the sea, and the sky. The music video featured the singer in soft-focus and slow-motion, caressing some anonymous female model, his real life homosexuality still an official secret at the time of the song's release.

Sebastian, Yonatan, and Kero ad-lib the lyrics and reduce the song's content to nonsense without changing the delivery, an earnest croon made to address no one about nothing, until they're all belting a kind of simulacra and s(t)imulation of romance. The three friends are even, briefly, in harmony.

Witching hour comes and the room packs with late-night regulars, mostly older goths and punks, some of the Jesuit brothers from the nearby parish, the community college theater club, and now that it's summer, a handful of that particular kind of tourist who pride themselves on seeking "authenticity" in their travels. Omens and Pour Tends is not on any visitor's guide, which is precisely its appeal for this type, usually single white dudes in their twenties and thirties, but also hippy couples, awkward graduate students of all stripes conspicuously looking for a narrative in their observations. Sometimes, even poets come, already three sheets to the wind and clearly hoping for something violent to occur so they can possess and decorate it, but there's rarely fights. There's never sports on the televisions. The staff are fearless, the regulars are friendly, and the rowdiest it ever gets is when the theater club kids bring new members to initiate and think everyone else is their captive audience. But nobody minds, really. One of the Jesuits is getting pretty good at darts, and he always claps politely for the singers.

The tourists stick out not in their appearances or their overt behavior, but how they carry their assumptions. Sebastian can always tell when someone comes to bask in the atmosphere of the dive. Their faces curl and glint with the masochism of standing too close to the blown-out speaker, finishing the odorous well draught, earning themselves a little bit of damage to escape their own minds but with a wink, like they were regular people trapped in the onslaughts of their daily lives and not jerks on vacation.

It gets later and then too late. Sebastian misses the last bus home until morning. He'll stay until Kero and Yonatan finish their shifts. His friends are busy during these peak hours, of course, so Sebastian has a lot of time to eat fried food and gently disassociate, or to watch who in the crowd watches him, and to contemplate the way his presence becomes the subject of others' contemplation.

He's not sure if he minds the tourists or not. They do spend a lot
of money. But he can almost hear his sister, Lara, laughing at the
onlookers, probably flashing them her boobs or flipping them off,
cackling at the exact kind of guy who thinks this is an invitation to
approach her, who doesn't know how good of a pick-pocket she is.
He can almost hear his brother, Oscar, demand to know what
someone is staring at, puff up his chest, stomp his huge feet, though
Oscar especially would never be here, and never will be.

Some part of Sebastian wants to tell these people, "I have
nothing against you, but *other* sorts of people, who are not here,
would steal your wallet and kick your butt all the way to Pizza Hut
if they were. I just think you should know that. Maybe you can put
it in your autobiographical road novel? But I don't know anything,
really. I'm only a local character. I'm the atmosphere. I'm the vibe.
By my very definition, I'm somewhat naive. Not creative in any
way. Not like you."

A scruffy, kind of waxy-looking guy with his collared shirt tucked
in and a yellow lanyard hanging from his back pocket comes in and
half-waves at Yonatan, orders an expensive sake. The man is
unfamiliar, but carries himself with less transience than tourists, so
must be new to the city for an office job that keeps him long hours.
Something thin, hard, and rectangular sits at the end of the lanyard,
an ID card for the job most likely, but Sebastian doesn't need to see
what it says to know the company. The particular shade of yellow is
trademarked. The color belongs to the same people, or entity, or
whatever they are, who are running the recruitment ads for the
moon, looking to staff it with the huddled masses yearning to break

into the bourgeois (or something like that; Sebastian is not sure).

Their logo is everywhere. Their name is a household one. But Sebastian resists speaking or writing it as much as he can. Power that omnipresent should not be permitted something as volatile as a name, not even a codename meant in parody. Taking God's name in vain was one thing. But there is no safety in naming mortal power, least of all to satirize it, when all the good that does is inspire the power to take you at your word, enact your dystopian exaggeration as their next move, turn your hell into your next reality.

Here is what to do instead:

1. Write down the longest verb you can spell, in any language, without a dictionary: _____.

2. Write down the last, family, or formal name of the worst boss you've ever had. Or if you, like Sebastian, have never been employed, choose any other authority figure who sticks in your memory like thorns through the palms of your hands; one who lacerated your motivation, you idealism, or your benefit of the doubt: _____.

3. Now take (a.) a syllable of choice from each word and write them together as a single bicapitalized word, or, (b.) if you're feeling that big pharma energy, with a hyphen, or, (c.) for a dash of software-as-a-service, drop consonants and swap vowels for emoji. Whatever it is your decide, write it down but keep it secret: _____.

And if you cannot keep a secret, you may still write it down, but then you must—you simply must—erase it immediately.

Give it a try in this following paragraph: _____ (fill in the blank) are establishing their second North American headquarters in Stella Maris following a years-long bidding war between cities across the continent, the governing bodies of each locale genuflecting before the promise of "jobs," courting with tax incentives and exemptions, ceding public lands, extending eminent domain to cede more than a few private ones as well.

Most people in Stella Maris are as surprised as anyone else to be the chosen site. Some are very angry. Some are very excited. And enough are trying to find hope and positivity in their lives to tune out the anger and ride the excitement instead.

It doesn't seem to matter what else _____ produces if it produces jobs; it started as an online-only clearinghouse for novelty infomercial products and light consumer gadgets, then it had campuses and outposts nationally, then globally, now extra-terrestrially, expanding to include a private mail service, a coffee shop franchise, a bank chain, weapons manufacturing, raw materials speculation, and a popular subscription box of shelf-stable food and nutrition supplements. Their business on the moon is vaguely described as "research."

But it also doesn't seem to matter to most people in Stella Maris what manner or quality of jobs this development entails, if there are a high enough quantity of them. Technically thousands of jobs appeared virtually overnight for the fancy, lucrative positions, but if Lanyard Guy is any indication, they were just as quickly filled by internal transfers. What's left are the contracts, the subcontracts, temping and testing and data entry and other garbage gigs, also some literal garbage gigs.

Exciting and rewarding opportunities for fools like Sebastian without any other option. He tries to help at last call, but he's slow with a mop, clumsy with the pint glasses. Ultimately not even his friends can in good faith recommend him for anything else.

"I am thinking about the moon thing?" he says.

"Yeah man! Do it!" Kero cheers and then yawns.

"Okay, but, *space*." Sebastian says. "I thought astronauts had to be decorated Air Force pilots as well as beloved science teachers who are also, um, in shape. To do space stuff you have to be amazing, like you would have to qualify for a hundred jobs."

"Not anymore you don't," Yonatan says. Yonatan does not sound tired, or hoarse, or otherwise at all like he's been working a bar all night. Sebastian stays awake with his friends for no real or good reason, but also the kind of no real or good reason that is on purpose, whereas Yonatan doesn't really sleep either way. He claims not to need more than a few hours for a nap each afternoon, and otherwise refuses to let his body "win."

"I just don't think I'm *allowed* in space," Sebastian realizes.

"Allowed? Trust me, Seb, they really don't care if you have a mental health thing. Probably don't care what condition you're in."

"No, I mean…" Sebastian trails off.

He thinks, hello, yes, his skills and qualifications are that he knows how to cross a floor of any material without making a sound. That he is quite adept at evading blows, for example to the face, for example he can cross his arms over his face in such a way that bruises can be hidden by long sleeves. That he is proficient at being anywhere and feeling like a visitor to a distant relative and that he should not touch anything. That he is an expert at crying for no reason, or used to be, though he hasn't cried at all in a long, long,

long, long time but that he is confident he could pick it back up again at any time, like riding a bicycle, as they say, though he wouldn't know, as he never learned to ride a bicycle. Or drive a car. Or swim. Since he's not supposed to go in the ocean past his chin, he's probably not allowed in space, either, at least not into the sky past the top floor of a building, really, and even then, only if he leaves enough room for the Holy Spirit between his restless, impulsive body and any open windows.

"I mean my mom," he says.

Yonatan nods. "Ah, right."

"Yeah, Donna would freeeeeak out about that, wouldn't she?" Kero finds the idea somehow irresistible.

"You could say that," Sebastian says.

"Then you should *definitely* do it!" Kero urges.

"Um. Do you guys want to get rid of me that badly?"

"Oh, honey," Yonatan says. "It's not like that."

"Yeah man, don't get it twisted," Kero says.

"Like, aren't these people the Bad Guys Du Jour and everything?"

"Eh," Yonatan shrugs his shoulders. "All the money's got blood on it if you look closely enough."

"You really think it doesn't matter?"

"It matters... My sincere opinion," Yonatan chews the words as he thinks aloud, spraying and wiping down the bartop. "Is that you should take the money, and do a bad job. Survive. If you get plucky, infiltrate, learn something you can keep, organize the other pawns and peons into a lunar labor collective. Or at least, don't be a scab if someone else takes that initiative. There is not really such a thing as selling out if you don't have much of a choice. Just don't let them break your heart."

"I guess." Sebastian is not relaxed enough to sigh, so he lets out a squeaky grunt instead. "I don't know."

The moon has always been there as a motif in art or a glow sticker on his bedroom ceiling, but now it grows, becomes the distant shore of his impending future, and the walls of Stella Maris are his mother. The border is her body. "Here" and "her" lose all meaningful distinction. Is he trapped? Could leaving a place ever really be an escape from it? Is what happened before still happening and will it happen again?

Time forms a circle, and then another circle along a different axis, and then another, until time is a mesh sphere pulsing through darkness to synthesizer arpeggios, a crude computer model on an old tape about the future, but the future in the video is from the past, and so everything collapses, flattens, and tomorrow and the days to come are already here, and you are certain of three fates at once:

1. You never leave home and never defy your mother.

2. You leave the entire planet in defiance of your mother.

3. Your mother is waiting for you on the moon when you arrive. She is in her pajamas and raises one of her slippers, hurls it at your head, and the slipper thwacks you in the face as she shouts about how dangerous this is, that you will definitely, absolute die if she doesn't kill you first, how since she made you that she can unmake you, how she saw you before you saw yourself, and meanwhile the slipper ricochets off your forehead and twirls off beyond the ends of the solar system, until aliens find it and study it to better understand human kind. And you cry out, please, yes, hello, your skills and qualifications for this exciting and rewarding

opportunity are that you still have a pulse, and you excel at forgetting entire years of your life, and laying in bed any time of day, and laying awake any time of night.

III.

When all three siblings still lived at home, about two or three years ago, they shared a single bedroom with a set of bunk beds and a trundle cot. Lara had the top bunk because she was the oldest, or at least that was the logic she used to justify her claim on the preferential bed, but the logic went uncontested. Oscar, as the middle child, had the lower bunk, but at least he could leverage seniority so that Sebastian had the cot.

Even after Oscar disappeared and Lara moved in with Maricel, Sebastian continued to sleep on the cot. The mattress was thin, barely an inch of yellow foam zipped into a crinkly waterproof fitted sheet, and the springs below sagged and started to give in to rust and strain, but it had sagged into the shape of his body after sleeping on it almost his entire life. The shape grew with him as he lengthened and widened into the largest member of their whole family.

Sebastian hit his growth spurt just as he'd begun to learn how to disappear, and then he no longer could. He gained all the presence of a giant pastel teddy bear strapped to the pop-up roof of a carnival game. Either a target, or a prize, maybe both. He moved like he didn't know how much room he took up, or like he might prefer to be a hologram or a laser beam or a little glass bird in a shadow box. He never learned any of the tactics of aggression, offensive or defensive, that Lara and Oscar inherited from their mother.

Not evasive like their father, either. Their father lived with them in only the most technical sense, sharing a home address, with occasional proximity between months-long travels for whatever it was he did for work, and when he was home it was as though he was unable to hear any of their voices. There were always voices, too, raised in every emotional state. Nothing that could be said simply within the same room was not shouted across the apartment instead. Their father could hear just fine, but chose not to. Sebastian was more attuned than that, and more fragile.

He couldn't grow facial hair. His voice dropped but still he spoke from high in his throat, sang practically from between his eyes, like letting air into his chest or oxygen in his lungs, so close to his heart, would catalyze an explosion. It was as though he was waiting for something better in the world around him before growing up completely within it, but what? What could possibly improve by holding your breath for twenty years? God only knew.

The siblings' bedroom had no windows except for a glass block set in the ceiling that slid in and out of a hole in the roof with a crude latch. Lara liked to leave it open in the summers, letting in a warm breeze and mosquitoes as large and twisted as corkscrews that assaulted the exposed planes of their bodies, or settled into the damp edges of the room. All of the siblings used the ceiling hole to climb up onto their roof, but it was no good for sneaking out beyond that. The roof was atop the thirteenth floor of their walk-up, a former boarding house with rust stains down one side in the shape of long-lost fire escapes, held together by a few hundred years of heavy beige paint inside and out, barely concealing mounting structural decay.

The room locked from the outside with an old-fashioned brass mechanical lock, and had no key, much less a passcode. The apartment came that way, or so their parents said, but the lock did look older than all of them. Lara thought the room had once been for storage or utilities, and maybe these top floor apartments were originally custodial instead of residential. Either way, it made confinement the natural state of things at home.

There was wall-to-wall carpet everywhere but the kitchen. The siblings wore a path in it with their whole bodies. And the rough pile of the carpet had, in turn, worn friction burns onto their legs, arms, necks, and backs where they had been pushed or dragged across it by the ear, by the hair, to avoid the swing of a shoe or a hand, after receiving it anyway.

What warranted these blows could be anything, really. Things that had been fine the day before, things that would become permissible the day after. What Lara, Oscar, and Sebastian shared, though it frayed each of them in such different ways, was the certainty of losing. Fear was something more basic than the bread of Communion, despair more automatic than reciting the "Our Father." It was inevitable. It was the tides. So it was not worthwhile to consider *if* the worst outcome would occur, only *when* it would occur next, because it always would.

The door broke once, when it was slammed shut from the outside at the same moment it was kicked out from the inside. There was every reason to replace it then, with a lighter door, a simpler door, a newer door. Something more typical of children's bedrooms. Even a bead curtain could have been worth what other teenagers might see as a loss of privacy. But their father fixed it, instead, on a weekend he was home, so the set patterns of the space were restored, preserved, maintained.

Some things are immune to insult but vulnerable to description. Lara had some choice words to describe her family. She looked up diagnostic manuals online. She would find a personal essay on some dynamic or disorder, be affirmed for an hour or two, and then search for another as soon as the righteousness ran dry, as though submerged in the depth of the internet there was clarity, ready for her, and waiting to be reached. A thread or a column or a comments section who could say, "I have seen your life and can confirm what you are experiencing is real, is bad, and here is what it's called, and you have done nothing wrong, so your soul is free now, and starting tomorrow, from now on until forever, you can feel better, at last."

When Lara first tried to call it as she saw it in heated moments, her mother might say, "You think this is so bad, huh? You have it too good. You're spoiled." Or, "Your grandfather would have used his belt." Or, "It's always your way or the highway. I hope someday you have children and they're exactly like you. Then you'll see."

Dad was there, too, but said nothing. Lara did press him once for a response, and just once, quiet and severe, he told her, "You won't be able to drive a wedge between your mother and I."

So Lara conspired with her brothers, tentative, at a whisper. The three of them were alone in their bedroom, that last summer they were all together. It was early in the morning. The tallow light of sunrise slipped into the dim night like powdered creamer into instant coffee.

Lara was trying to reframe her thoughts as questions, particularly around subjects she was an expert on. She didn't like to play dumb, but tactically, she had started to feel out the power of leading others to believing they had come to her conclusions on their own.

"Do you guys ever think maybe our parents are abusive?"

Oscar scoffed. Sebastian made a crackling noise, a sort of hesitant croak for a moment, considering the question, and then said, "I don't think so?"

"What?" Lara heard him just fine, but did not accept the answer. But she tried once more to pretend that she simply didn't understand. "Why not?"

"It's not like I feel awesome, exactly, about some of the stuff." Sebastian did not specify what the stuff was, or who did it, or even that it happened to him. "But *abusive* feels like too strong a word?"

"Yeah, Lars," Oscar said. His impatience was palpable; Lara could sense him rolling his eyes through the stuffy dark texture of the air. Lars was the nickname Lara had asked everyone to use for her when she was fourteen, and since recanted, but Oscar continued to use it precisely because, by then, it just embarrassed her. "Families fight with each other. It's normal."

"I feel like, maybe, it seems like a strong word because it's accurate, and that's scary," Lara said.

"Some people kill their kids," Oscar countered. "Some parents are actual monsters. You ever read about the lady that cut off her baby's arms? Or the guy whose wife tried to leave him so he shot all their children and told her to live and suffer?"

"That's disgusting." Apparently Lara wasn't the only one obsessively researching her interests online. Oscar sounded more and more like one of those edgelords who gets really into serial killers.

"We're intact, yeah?" Oscar continued. "We eat enough, don't we? You sure as hell do."

"Shut the fuck up!" Lara snapped. But Oscar did not. So much for the passive approach.

"Look. We can read, and tie our shoes, and nobody got left behind at the mall or thrown into the deep end. Plus it's not like any of us have been through half of what mom and dad have. You know what things were like back when they met, right? There was real, actual violence. They're doing their best."

"Someone can do their best and it can still not be good enough." Lara was suddenly tired. It was too early to be talking. It was too early to be awake. She wished she could fall back asleep and wake up an only child.

"Wow, deep." Oscar kicked the underside of Lara's bunk. "Why are you always looking for attention in the most retarded ways?"

"Hardship doesn't excuse treating other people like crap!"

"Yes it does, moron," Oscar sighed. "You fucking idiot. Of course it does." He got up and made to get dressed.

"I just want someone other me to acknowledge reality!" Lara raised her voice just short of yelling. She had thought her brothers, despite their differences, would be her natural witness for this *one* thing, if nothing else in the universe.

"Cool, well, good luck with that," Oscar replied. He never really changed out of pajamas and into clothes since he always slept in his clothes, but he'd thrown on his bomber jacket and canvas shoes. He rummaged through his dresser drawer. Lara couldn't see what he grabbed from within it but it clacked in his hands and fit into a jacket pocket. He let himself out and shut the bedroom door behind him as slow and quiet as possible. Muffled falls of his sneakers on the kitchen tile, then the click and groan of the front door. Lara pictured him stepping into the rot-ridden hallway, the sounds of him absorbed by the padding of slime or mold or mildew or whatever it all was. Lara had this image of Oscar crushing the spores under his heels, beheading the mushrooms that peered from the clapboard of the walls with his jagged fingernails, but the growths—bile black and mucus green and fever red—simply repairing themselves around his feet and hands, overtaking him, until all of Oscar was assimilated to the colony and melted away, waiting for the next rain, ready to explode.

Sebastian made a sharp inhale through his nose, held it, let out one of his signature grunts that sounded like a question.

"But. So. Like," he started. "So, my tics and anxiety and stuff have been getting pretty bad, right? And yeah, I guess mom feels like she has to tell me I'm on the Crazy Train to Axe Murderer Town and dad I guess agrees."

"See, this is my point," Lara interrupted, but Sebastian barreled on.

"Last week, mom took me to this place where there's a lady in the front who talks to ghosts and exorcises demons and then in the back is the pharmacy with the real old-timey soda fountain but the soda flavors are like cough syrups and stuff like that," Sebastian said. His words came tumbling out, one right on top of the next, and Lara flinched and leaned over her bed towards him, as if she might dive and catch them in her hands. "Or maybe it is just soda but it tastes really bad and herbal so it feels like it's healthy. So we went in through the front and I thought the medium was gonna slap me with holy water but instead we talked for a bit and she sort of stared at me and then at mom and wrote me a scrip and pointed us to the back. And at first I thought mom was angry at me for not having a quicker or like a permanent fix, because you know how she sulks when she's embarrassed? I guess she had just finished with work and she was tired. But then the pharmacist said the meds were going to cost pretty much one-hundred percent of our food money? The medium lady was nice but the pharmacist was sort of trying to get rid of us, I think. He was explaining how expensive it all was and how there was nothing he could do, but in that way where there definitely was something he could do? Because mom was in her work scrubs and I was in sweatpants, you know? And the school Spirit Day tee shirt that has a burn hole in it, even though it wasn't my fault that I fell on a lit candle when I had that blackout. So the pharmacist must have been, like, oh you people can't have this, right? People like you can't afford it, you'll probably just sell it. He was being a gatekeeper but like an actual, literal barrier to access and everything, not a gatekeeper like, you know, someone on the internet who is rude but it doesn't really affect you. But then it was like. Mom talked him down!"

"What, did she speak to the manager or something?"

"She didn't have to! All she did was use her Mom Voice."

Lara mock-shuddered. "Yeah, I know the one."

"Right! But, um. So. She scolded him for being mean to us and profiteering off the health and well-being of children, and for a moment I was confused until I remembered I was a child technically, but I could see him straighten up and just sort of. Obey. From the most lizard brain, tiny-baby part of him. Then he was the child and she was disappointed in him and he was going to either cry or give her what she wanted, so he gave us a discount on a three-month supply and set me up on an automatic refill."

"Right," said Lara. "Cause no one is allowed to bully us but her."

Sebastian fell silent. Lara felt under her pillow for her phone, grabbed it, then pulled her comforter over her head like a mortician's sheet. Every single thing on her social media was annoying. The news was annoying. At least she was done with schoolwork forever and ever, good riddance, amen. She read an advice column, then the front page of a music site, and then followed a scattering of jokes and call out posts from mutuals of mutuals, back to a complete stranger's meltdown and the apparent implosion of a fandom the stranger was hugely active in. Some British fantasy miniseries where people went extra hard shipping two characters who turned out to be fraternal twins. The original poster had built an argument about how twincest slash was an important part of their trauma recovery but they didn't exactly say what the trauma was, and there was this whole cycle of adjacent thinkpieces and subtweets about whether or not to make people divulge their worst experiences as a credential to speak about things, and then a bunch of kink people got involved because nobody had further questioned assuming fetishes were always by default the result of negative trauma, and then it surfaced that the original poster was an only child and had stalked and sexually harassed someone they claimed was their long lost sibling separated at birth, and they had tried to delete the evidence but the screencaps were surfacing in the comments of the fandom wiki. It just kept *going*. Lara sent some of the juicer bits to her friend Nicole who basically lived for messy internet drama with only the comment, "phew!"

Lara hadn't even watched the show the fandom was based around. She hated anything set in London, even magical fantasy London (maybe especially magical fantasy London), but really anything with posh accents. It just seemed so over-done. Who gave a shit if wizards and royalty lived or died when their entire social system was inherently corrupt?

But now she was out of distractions and still feeling like garbage and it was still way too early to get up. Sebastian's breathing was shallow but even. She assumed he'd dozed back off. She texted Maricel.

LARA:	hey, are you awake yet?
LARA:	mariiiiiiiceeellllll
LARA:	mari
LARA:	look so like
LARA:	shit is just getting worse here
LARA:	like my mom was already a psycho bitch but now shes a triple bitch mega psycho
LARA:	hose beast
LARA:	my brothers are little bitches they think im overreacting
LARA:	im literally going to die if im in this apartment another day
LARA:	ill get a less shitty job and become a big crazy workaholic if it means we can look at some actual places
LARA:	i have to get out of here
MARICEL:	Ah sorry honey!! I didn't see these messages until just now!
MARICEL:	I was asleep

LARA: i love you so much

MARICEL: I'm sorry it's so fucked up right now.

LARA: run away with me

LARA: i mean like to the other side of town or something
            but for real

LARA: we keep joking about a place together

LARA: lets just do it

MARICEL: You're serious?

LARA: yes!!!

MARICEL: I dunno baby...

LARA: mari please im begging you

LARA: im going to probably kill myself if i dony

LARA: * dont get out of here

MARICEL: Don't do anything drastic, please!

MARICEL: We can't kiss if you're dead! :(

MARICEL: The moving thing is just a little fast for me. I don't
            feel like we're there yet? But I really want to be
            there with you! The imagining itself is really fun
            for me.

LARA: mari i love you

LARA: there is no way that will ever change

LARA: i really need this

LARA: i cant wait anymore

LARA: mari please

LARA: mari im dying

LARA: maricel? hello?

MARICEL: Can we talk about it later? I'm really tired right
            now.

LARA: omg sorry yes later is fine

LARA: youre fucking incredible im just being nuts lol

LARA: i cant believe how lucky i am

LARA: love you love you love you

Maricel's icon went gray and her name fell from the bright and bold ACTIVE NOW to the second tier of ACTIVE RECENTLY. Lara knew she could be kind of intense but Maricel must have known she could drag her feet about obviously good ideas, too. Once they got an apartment together, everything was going to be so perfect. Lara didn't care what she had to do to make it work. No one else would be around to tell them no, and that was priceless.

"Sometimes, I think it's not that our parents are bad at being parents," Sebastian said, and Lara yelped.

"Have you just been laying there awake staring at me this whole time?"

"I was thinking about what you said," Sebastian continued. His speech slower and more reverent than before. "Like, our parents are not bad in general, absolute terms, so much as we happen to be incompatible. Like, maybe they'd be excellent parents to an easier kid, or if I was better, you know? But instead they got me, and I'm a lot, and I know I'm a lot."

"It doesn't work like that." Whatever the thing was that Lara was feeling was not anger anymore. Not even fear. It had writhed and boiled alive in her chest, and now it floated dead in her stomach. She fussed with the ceiling block, let in bugs and noise and the morning fog.

"Okay," Sebastian replied. "I'll try to think about that, too, I guess. I'm trying to be better."

"Going for sainthood, huh?"

"Something like that."

The fog filled their bedroom through the tiny window. It was verdant-gray. It was like an astral projection, the way the ocean lifted off itself and rolled over the city in billowing curtains. The Atlantic climate was hyper-real no matter the weather. Every time the temperature or humidity or light shifted, their neighborhood looked like the over-airbrushed cover of a supermarket novel. The genre depended on the season. Summer was a political thriller, fall a murder mystery, winter a blue-collar historical romance, and spring one of those inspirational pulps where the stranger who comes to town is always a guardian angel and rain falls as a baptism. Anything that billed itself as authentic in Stella Maris was, of course, a highly curated tourist trap. So what did it matter, anyway, about reality and fantasy, when everything that was in fact unique or natural or genuinely experienced was that much more the stage magic, that much further away?

IV.

The fog got so thick crawling up the mouth of the Immaculate River, in particular, and loomed over its banks, that the river was said to be haunted. The mud slurped like a hungry mouth and tugged at your ankles, though many swore it was not the mud but clinging little hands grasping from beneath. Orbs of light appeared over the water, especially at night. Sound carried backwards. If someone called your name from behind you, higher on the banks, you would hear it as though coming from the other side of the river, tempting you closer to the water's edge. Lara knew that her mother, Donna, had been warned not to play there as a girl, even in the daytime. There were too many stories of young children meeting new playmates in the haze, other children they had never seen before, who were eager to show them the river's unseen bottom and keep them there.

Lara knew only a few things for certain about her mother's life before her, like that Donna was born in Stella Maris and would likely live there her entire life, like Pop-pop and Nana before her. Before them, Donna's many varied grandparents and great-grandparents came to the area same as tens of thousands of others did in the Eighteen-Hundred-and-Industrialization times: from elsewhere, to work in the mills and factories that surged along and over the Immaculate, powered by the current. The water flowed in through turbines and out through waste and exhaust pipes that brought inventive new colors and temperatures and textures to the river's ecosystem.

Lara knew that her mother's first job was running errands for the fried clam shacks along the boardwalks, back when there were still clams safe to eat, or at least before the consequences of eating them were more immediate. Nineteen-Midcentury-Seven. Lara knew the story well because her mother told it every time they got new winter clothes. Donna started with how she had been eleven or maybe twelve, "all legs," and paid in cigarettes and tips to run bread rolls from the bakeries downtown to the cramped clam shack short-order griddles where they'd be cut, buttered, toasted, and overstuffed with crispy shellfish or scrod, tossed in mayonnaise and lemon juice, salt and pepper, coleslaw, pickles, spicy relish. Lara's mother had been the oldest of seven, and back then Pop-pop decided she was growing too fast for one who couldn't be clothed in hand-me-downs. Pop-pop's new rule was: either stop growing, or buy your own clothing.

Lara's mother sometimes said that she had, due to this rule, gone two winters without a coat before she got the job; sometimes the story was that Pop-pop hadn't really meant it and just wanted her out of the house when she wasn't in school; always the story trailed towards an anecdote that cigarettes give eleven-or-twelve-year-olds a ton of energy to run bags of hot bread four miles round trip by foot, and the lesson that before the first frost that year, Donna bought herself a coat.

"A navy blue pea coat with red lining and brass buttons from Sears—you wouldn't remember malls but they used to have big flagship stores like that—and it was *brand* new, not even on sale." Donna was always proud of that last fact.

The bread route cut along the banks of the river most of the way there and back, and sometimes Donna swore that she did see ghosts.

"Oh, plenty of times."

Lara's mother was a young adult before the official view of the city was that the river was not haunted, merely so polluted that it could have and had caused hallucinations and "might" fatally affect swimmers and bathers, children in particular, and correlated with a number of health complications in general for the mill workers and their families who lived in the tenements adjacent to the water. By then, deindustrialization was well underway; the factories were closing and leaving the river people with little else but cancer and ghost stories.

Lara had heard about how there was a youth movement back then, that wanted to bring together the workers and the environmentalists, and that her mother got involved. They were working on fixing the job situation as well as the pollution situation. They said things like, "No justice, no peace," but maybe they didn't, because often Donna quoted this slogan to frame her own intentions: "Mostly, I just wanted a job, and didn't care what kind anymore."

Lara's mother supposedly met Lara's father at a meeting where her father admitted aloud, "Either justice or peace would be fine, to be honest." Lara could not imagine him saying it, and suspected that Donna had made this up to condense and fabricate the truth of how the couple got together. They had met and married quickly, that was verifiable.

On some level, both of Lara's parents married because they were each ready to compromise. It seemed if you asked for something simple enough, "just a spouse," "just a job," just one thing at a time, it was somehow more practical, more humble, more likely to work out or prove workable.

Lara's mother said that she found the theory-heavy activists obnoxious, and Lara discerned that this was sometimes because the people her mother described as such didn't know what they were talking about, and sometimes because they did, very much, and were prepared to ask for the world and everything in it at once. Donna might say that those sorts of demands seemed wonderful, and like a great prelude to "be disappeared in the middle of the night." Donna sometimes asked if idealists "understood that it wasn't about exposing the truth." That it "wasn't about gold or armies or pulling up railroad spikes anymore." That a private security sub-contractor could "have you vaporized by remote control."

Yet Donna also, sometimes, told how she had surprised herself. How she found a little work cleaning houses for the city's small but steady circle of wealth—the industry was gone but, like the illnesses and the ghosts, the heritable trusts and estates it produced remained —yet she continued to attend the meetings. Donna learned about all manner of tactics, and then trained in them, and then trained others in them.

Donna told Lara that someone (sometimes a stranger, sometimes Lara's father) once asked her, "How do you know any of it going to do anything?" and that Donna had replied, "I don't," but that it wasn't an admission of doubt; it was a counter-challenge. Things were getting serious. Public sentiment was in their favor back then. They might even have achieved what they set out to do. Plus, Donna was pregnant—"This is where you come in, since I know that's what you're waiting for"—which was turning out to be a miserable experience sustained by a belief in what was yet to come. And Donna might admit that when a lot of her friends had burned out or moved on, fixed their immediate problems or stopped caring, that a lot of "those utopian wackos" were surprisingly reliable for meal trains. Donna still wasn't sure that she liked them, but when Lara was born, she had to trust them, because she couldn't argue with their casseroles.

Donna might tell her children that she worked her entire life, and this might be the only consistent story that she ever told them. Donna might joke that she used to be political when she was younger, but that it didn't pay. Sometimes she said this and laughed at some additional joke happening privately, unspoken, and sometimes she said it with the suggestion of resentment, or regret, or defiance. She had a limp, and her children could plainly see that she had some kind of injury to her knees, and a speckle of funny-shaped scars on her lower back and sides. She would not talk about how she got them.

"Your mama wrestled bears," she might say. Or, "I was stung by a thousand bees." But these deflections were never followed by laughter or anger or any kind of clue, just these brief and deadpan fairy tales that brought the conversation to its end, and once Lara was too old to accept the magic animal tales, her mother stopped answering the question altogether.

The boys learned not to be so curious (or, their mother might say, so nosy), but Lara never let up asking questions again and again if she was unsatisfied with any of the previous answers.

Her mother wanted her oldest and her only daughter to be strong, and smart, too, but not like *that*.

Donna would issue warnings about living in a man's world. She might say, "The woman always gets left holding the bag," and Lara would decry the injustice, but to her mother, she was "always finding ways to be offended" and make it somehow Donna's fault. Maybe it was true, Lara considered, that girls unfairly held women responsible for their roles, but their betrayals stung twice than those of men, somehow. Donna tensed and tuned out as soon as Lara said anything about "feminism" or "misogyny" or "patriarchy." And yet, it was also her mother who would laugh and comment on the lack of substance in things like *International Working Women's Day*.

"Oh, is it a holiday, for me?" Donna would say. "Then where's my overtime pay?"

Donna encouraged her daughter to foster close, non-competitive relationships with other girls, but was openly and unambiguously disappointed when Lara did precisely this by dating a few of them. Lara's mother tried to sway her back a bit. She might say, "Everyone goes through that phase where they have a crush on their friends, but you get over it." And Lara would dig her heels in deeper still.

"No they don't, mom. What are you trying to tell me?"

And Donna might say, "If you need to feel smarter than me so badly, you should get better grades in school."

Other days it was Lara's weight. Lara was fat, and Donna was "just worried" about her health. And Lara would insist, "I'm fine. I like the way I am," which confused her mother at best, but it might throw her off from escalating the issue for a little while.

In a less careful mood, Lara would point out, "Literally this whole family is fat. You're fat, too."

And Donna might say, "That's different. I had three children." Or instead, she might say, "I used to be thin, you know. People were nicer to me. I just want you to have what I didn't." Or she might lament a recalled line of appetite suppressants she used to enjoy, like it were a discontinued favorite flavor of ice cream. Or she might choose the worst option, Lara felt, and wallow.

Donna hid small pieces of candy around the apartment for herself to find. She retold a particular joke whenever she re-discovered one. "If you break it in half, the calories fall out!" And when Lara was tired of trying to convince her to just enjoy the fucking chocolate, already, Lara would complain that Donna had retold the joke yet again, and volunteer that "nobody found it funny." But Donna always did. If she could laugh at her own stale jokes about eating and weight then there was still somewhere in her relationship to food for delight.

There was not a day under the same roof that they were unable to find a way to hurt one another, inclusive of the day Lara announced that she was moving in with Maricel on the complete opposite end of town.

Donna pretended to forget Maricel's name most of the time. She pretended to think the word "girlfriend" meant a friend who was a girl, even though that usage hadn't been common since her own mother was young. "Lara's new roommate," she might say instead, even after it had been several years.

But Donna still called her daughter once or twice a week, receiving no answer more often than not. She always left a voicemail, asking if Lara was okay, talking around Oscar's absence, impatient with whatever was the matter with Sebastian. If Lara's youngest brother ever did move out, too, he was moving deeper inward first.

Aloud in her messages, mostly deleted unheard, Donna wondered where, along the way, she had gone wrong? All of her children, for who she would move Heaven and Earth, though they could never appreciate the depths of her sacrifices for them, were abandoning her.

v.

When Lara left home, she'd waited until a morning that everyone else was out, and took all of her possessions, plus a few of "common" ones as well. Some, but not all, of the good dishes; a laundry basket; towels; batteries. Lara never outright *stole*, per se, but she carefully stockpiled things nobody would miss. Discarded things, abandoned things, overlooked things, but most of all, extraneous things. Some people had more than they needed, and more than they knew they needed, and she never took from any other kind of person. Fair? Maybe or maybe not. But just? Of course.

Now, as she carted desert platters into the ballroom of the Hotel Saint Langrenus, and set out an abundance of osprey egg custards in platinum bowls, seaweed tarts on tiered porcelain trays, and snail mousse in miniature crystal flutes, she palmed mint creams and chocolates into her apron.

The silver chandeliers dimmed and the milk-glow of moonlight and neon poured through the grand springline windows of the ballroom. A man holding a bottle of champagne under one arm and a high-end amateur telescope under the other took to the stage beneath the windows. Unlike most of the attendees in their eveningwear and cocktail finery, he wore a fleece vest and dirty running shoes with total confidence, but not the oblivious confidence of someone with nothing to prove. Cockiness, really. It was clear from the other end of the room, in the shadows of shoving dishes around, what sort of power move he played with every wrinkle in his casual slacks.

Lara and the other caterers arranged the last of the deserts onto the white banquet tables as the man set down the bottle to set up the telescope in a conspicuous show of self-sufficiency. This high floor of the hotel had to be the best view of city center and the Gulf of

Seven Sorrows from within Stella Maris proper. The man pointed his lens right at the enormous full moon. Lara rarely saw a more inviting scene, as if she could step through the windows, take to the skyline like a catwalk, and strut right over the water and onto the surface of the satellite. The man peeked through his viewfinder, grimaced, and adjusted the tilt higher still.

He tapped on his Adam's apple and a wet grunt from his throat boomed through the hotel sound system. A diffuse pool of light rose over the stage and the room's conversations, negotiations, and networking fell to an attentive silence.

He did not introduce himself, and did not need to. He asked a rhetorical question, then answered it with an over-wrought punchline. Dude had the weirdest energy, darting around the stage like a helicopter drone, with these oversized expressions on his face as if a Christmas carol might burst out of his mouth any moment now, but his eyes were glassy and tunneling, with all the same focus and all the same hunger as a bird of prey.

A screen lowered from the ceiling where his slides flashed into view, and the vista of the city was left in view on either side, scaffolding him, enclosing him, like a setting for a crown jewel. His presentation began with the textbook stock image of Iacomo di Santa Sede "discovering" and founding Stella Maris, as if Ol' Jack had been intending for his ship to wash up here when he went treasure hunting, and all the indigenous people simply evaporated like dew drops. The next slide was a telescopic picture of the moon before it had been developed, with the presenter photoshopped in like he was "discovering" it in the same way. The moon was just a bald, naked rock for a zillion years, minding its own business.

Though now that it was crusted with buildings, it was hard to imagine it without them.

Stella Maris meant "star of the sea," a name for the Virgin Mary that was so old it was probably a mistranslation or misunderstanding of something else entirely. The man made a rehearsed "sea to the stars" joke. He talked about how exciting a time it was for both shareholders and "average, hard-working families," in the same breath, a little public relations magic to keep people who were screwed-over and tired feeling sort of ennobled about their toil and full of warm camaraderie towards the people screwing them over.

Lara rubbed her eyes so she could roll them and pass it off as regular exhaustion. No matter the industry, these executive types slobbered from the same dog dish of bullshit and expected everyone to smell charisma on their breath.

Lara and the other caterers quietly carted the dinner dishes and leftovers from the night's previous courses to the back of the ballroom, where they opened brushed steel panels along the wall and slid a remarkable number of untouched appetizers and half-nibbled entrees into a circuit of continuous dumbwaiters. Lara wanted to ask the banquet attendees if they were aware that they had bodies. Probably not. These creeps had ordered the hotel's most elaborate catering package and barely ate, though they certainly drank and drank some more.

Lara stole a glance at the faces in the audience. Generic, maybe generated by algorithm or committee. Were they robots, maybe? But one of them returned her a pissy look right back. Not robots then. Robots were nicer, and did not usually put back this much wine.

Lara's stomach rumbled. She snatched a pristine bread roll and packet of soup crackers with one hand, letting it slide right up into her sleeve as she continued to load dishes, and with her other hand, she groped into the pockets of her uniform and checked her phone. They were definitely not supposed to get caught looking at anything more than a watch on the floor, but Lara needed a boost. She felt a small, reliable rush from the notifications waiting for her attention. Two texts from Maricel.

MARICEL: HI HONEY 🐾

MARICEL: How's the Robber Baron's Ball or whatever? Haha

LARA: pretty restrained reception vibe for a bunch of settler colonialist gentrifying war criminals out to conquer the moon!!!

LARA: everyone leave the moon alone!

LARA: leave space alone, actually

LARA: she doesn't want us there

LARA: it's against the rules on an existential/moral/ethical level to try and live there and you go immediately to hell if you try to profit off it

MARICEL: We really should not put people in space

MARICEL: We are not water bears

LARA: hahaha right?

The man concluded his spiel by bracing the champagne bottle between his thighs and jerking out the cork with his bare hands. It popped into the vaulted ceiling of the ballroom and the crowd cheered, stood, and applauded.

Lara glanced toward the service hallway and tech tables at back-of-house. The miserable fuck commonly known as the catering supervisor was headed over. Lara climbed into a dumbwaiter behind a trash dolly as casually as possible, which was not very much, but she put on her best Helpful Voice and assured a few bemused coworkers that she was "just taking out the trash" as the panel groaned shut. She delighted that her body and the full bags of garbage even shared a certain shape and heft. They lumbered together down the hundred stories. She could probably wear one and sneak out in disguise like a cartoon sight gag.

There's wasn't great reception in the freight shafts but Lara continued the chat with Maricel.

MARICEL:	Ughhhh I miss yooooouuu 👻
MARICEL:	Can't you get a day off?
LARA:	i'm stockpiling forbidden breads
LARA:	next time we hang we feast as queens
MARICEL:	Lara the klepto rebel punk
MARICEL:	Ⓐ ⚐ ∞ ✊ ✊ ✊ ✊
MARICEL:	I'm certain that capitalism will be overthrown this time by petty theft
LARA:	LOOK
LARA:	you won't find it so funny when it's the apocolypse
LARA:	and we're holed up in the best bunker in the outlands where I have stored my MANY various toasts
LARA:	maybe some cough drops, tea, pillows, stress balls
LARA:	apocalypses can be very dry and stressful! exhausting really
MARICEL:	HAHA on that note I'm going to bread
MARICEL:	Bed! GOING TO BED fucking autocorrect

The dumbwaiter cranked to a stop and opened to the back of the ground floor, where the very same catering supervisor she moved to dodge stood waiting between the loading docks and the dumpsters.

"*How?*" She blurted it out before she could stop herself. He had an unbroken record of appearing when and where Lara most wanted to be unobserved, as if by no effort on his part. She fumbled her phone back into her apron and pushed the trash dolly out onto the concrete ramps.

"That better be work-related business on there, Miss Lara," he said. He didn't even sound angry or surprised. Worse, he sounded friendly.

"Yes, sir," Lara said. He was one of those slick dicks who knew better than to try anything *directly* like a regular pervert and so had adapted by leering through managing, horny *specifically* for getting people in trouble.

She wheeled the trash dolly down through plastic strip curtains to the pen of dumpsters. One of the casters dragged and spun, making it impossible to lead the dolly in a straight line, and the catering supervisor watched Lara struggle with it for another moment. The individual wrappings of the candies she'd stashed rustled conspicuously when she twisted and heaved herself against the load.

"Since you've evidently volunteered for dump duty," he continued. "We've had some hotel and client property go missing this evening, and I wondered if you might know where it's been misplaced?"

"No," Lara said. One by one, she lifted the bags of discarded food and tossed them over the rail. The soups, dressings, gravies, and sauces leaked, dribbled, and slapped the bottom of the dumpsters like an industrial-sized chunk blow.

"Oh, nothing? Not some banquet food and garnishes that never quite made it to either our clients, who rightfully paid for it, or the trash, where it otherwise belongs?"

"Nope." When Lara got to the wine bottles, she threw them in two at a time, working up a rhythm like a taiko drummer.

"Hmm," he mocked. "Both stealing and lying are not a good look for a young woman."

Lara pulled a spray bottle of bleach from off the side of the dolly and misted the mess inside the dumpster. It was the hotel's mandatory procedure against "wild animals," but Lara never saw any in this area. Just street people slinking from one hideout to another.

The catering supervisor took a step towards her. "You'll let me know immediately if and when you do remember, won't you?" He moved closer still, and Lara's whole body clenched, almost in pain to the anticipation of unwanted touch. She'd come down for solitude but now she was *alone*.

Some instinct took over and Lara turned, faced the catering supervisor, and pointed the nozzle of the bleach spray at his face, still holding the trigger.

"Of course," she said, and though it was her voice in her throat, it was a menacingly cold and certain and primal version of her voice. It was The Mom Voice.

The cadence of it was familiar, the command of the words said and implied like a song she had heard so many times that she knew both the tune and the lyrics without ever meaning to memorize them.

And something left within the catering supervisor's psyche understood it, too. The lost child buried within the troglodyte crust. He sputtered less than half of a syllable, flinched fast enough to miss, but after this half of a half-moment, he surrendered, wished her a good evening, and left.

Lara was tired of wasting her time doing dumb shit for assholes. It really had been months since she and Maricel actually went on date or any of the cute little adventures they used to do when they started dating.

She reached to message her girlfriend again, knowing full well the vibration of Maricel's phone would keep her awake—of course she knew; her problem was never lack of self-awareness but the sheer extent to which she would rationalize her actions and feelings that she was so aware of—and then she stopped, and didn't touch the phone at all.

Lara felt for once that, actually, anything in the world that she wanted, she could eventually get, because she could wear down the boundaries of her friends as much as the resolve of her enemies.

She was turning into her mother. Fuck fuck fuck fuck fuck FUCK.

Lara closed up the dumpsters and hopped down into the parking lot to clear her nostrils. She could evaporate right into the steam off a sewer grate. She got into her car and veered up onto the overpass towards home.

It was a forty-minute drive all together. Better than her old commute. In the dark, she knew she was nearing home by the shrinking store fronts. A supermarket became a few bodegas, a large bank became a pawn shop and a check cashing kiosk.

At checkpoints, guards scanned identity cards by circumnavigating the idling cars on foot. Lara flashed hers in the window without looking up. She knew the rhythm of the night guards by now, could sense the slightest gesture of acknowledgment in her peripheral vision. Usually it was half way between a blink and a nod, but the guard on this night was newer, still kept up a light dance of pointing, thumbs up, fluttering all of his fingers to summon someone for follow up questions. He'd exhaust himself soon enough, find that the whole routine could be performed on a level of microgestures, the smallest lingering glance.

Conflict, should it arise, Lara was ready for. There was no one in the world who could scare her more than her mom, and if she was becoming the force that hurt her the most, then there really was nothing left, based in reality, that should bother her. Or this was how people became shitty to their girlfriends, by spending all day being shitty, period, to get by.

The rookie try-hard checkpoint guard wanted to inspect the contents of her car. In a moment he would probably find the hotel food. Lara was not worried. She would code switch, argue, fawn, dodge, whatever, and if all of that didn't work and someone came for her after all, over a pile of pastries, Lara figured she could always humiliate them. There was a way to say practically anything in a certain tone that could make a person feel like a toddler in trouble with their mother.

VI.

Are you there Sebastian?

It's me.

Sorry I've been kind of distant lately. The reason for that is that I've been kind of distant lately.

Follow my instructions. Message one of the contact codes from the recruitment materials. A billboard, a targeted ad, a commercial, it doesn't matter. They all take you to the same inbox. Receive the automated response with the link that says "get started."

Get started. Install their proprietary software. It's a personality assessment. It really is that long. Maybe the duration screens out anyone who isn't serious about serving a global community for flexible pay. Maybe it's just a way for them to better understand your judgment and ability to sort important information from unimportant information.

Press acknowledge. The light on your phone's camera and microphone pulse blue. They are recording you taking the test, to ensure that you don't cheat by looking up answers about your own judgment and ability to sort important information from unimportant information. Maybe they analyze the feed in real time. Maybe they have those graphics analysis AIs that can tell them about your vital statistics, or if your face matches the face on any watch-list, or what your expression implies about your intentions.

NOTE: You may now begin the first section (Basic Information).

NOTE: Check all that apply.

Q: What is your name?
     _ Yes.
     _ No.

Q: What is your age?
     _ Like, twelve.

_ Youth.

_ Old enough to know better.

_ Vanishing into obscurity.

Q: Are you a robot?

_ No, I am not a robot.

_ I'm unsure.

_ Cyborg (Registered).

_ Cyborg (Unregistered).

_ Android, Virtual Assistant, or Electronic Companion.

Q: What is your race?

_ Passively invested in structural inequality through ethno-nationalism.

_ Actively invested in structural inequality through ethno-nationalism.

_ Passively resistant to structural inequality through ethno-nationalism.

_ Actively resistant to structural inequality through ethno-nationalism.

_ Guilty, confused, opportunistic, and/or defensive about this question.

_ Actually it's about fairness in video games journalism.

Q: Optional but strongly encouraged: How do you identify?

_ Goth.

_ Prep.

_ Jock.

_ Nerd.

_ Top.

_ Bottom.

_ Verse.

_ Selfie.

_ Cranky.

_ Furry.

_ Hexagon.

_ Everything but rap and country.

_ Womxn, womyn, fem/me (including fatal-spectrum), bimb@, or sugar baby.

_ Call me Cis Male. Some years ago—a lady never tells —having no cash, no class, and neither gas, ass, nor grass to pay my way around the old count-ray, I went to sea for a fee and to see if the sea would agree with me. Anchors a-weigh for pay; it is a way I have of driving off panic attacks and a very long list of other ailments and self-diagnoses. Anyway, I got gone; I prayed, got paid; I did not get laid. With a philosophical flourish, I sashayed to the ship. If they but knew it, almost all men, women, enbees, robots, and probably dogs, in their degree, some time or other, are horny for the ocean, which is our collective wife. This is also the extent of my bisexuality.

NOTE: You have completed the first section (Basic Information), and may proceed to the second section (Quantitative Reasoning).

Q: If you brother sneaks out between 10:00PM and
     4:00AM an average of four (4) nights a week after
     arguing with your mother at a volume of x decibels,
     and has taken to swimming in open water after Y
     alcoholic beverages in a fog with an average thickness
     of Z, what is the likeness that one morning he will
     simply not return, and with what percent confidence
     would you suspect his disappearance to be deliberate?
     Consider additional factors such as these: that he is
     known as a strong swimmer, that he is known to
     admire several vigilante groups that pass through the
     outlands beyond the city walls, that he took his gun
     but not his wallet with him when he left, that his neck
     tattoos would serve as unique identifying markers
     were he either locally disguised or deceased, that the
     line work of the tattoos are blue, that it is the same
     blue as the robe and veil of the Virgin?
     _   The quadratic formula.
     _   The golden ratio.
     _   The answer to this question is not a valid integer.

Q: Suppose that an explorer boards a galleon headed west
     across the Atlantic, at a maximum speed of nine knots
     but an average speed of five knots. Suppose he
     possesses an out-dated map which indicates the
     trajectory of a floating island off the coast of the New
     World, somewhere between the Chesapeake Bay and

the Saint Lawrence River.

The island is said to have black sand and lost treasures from every sea-faring civilization. The island is said to be strewn, as well, with skeletons. Among the pebbles and the gold are the blanching bones of men and women who followed the call of sirens or mermaids or their own death wish, or so it is said. It may also be said that they are the bones of those who have been kidnapped, enslaved, thrown or leapt overboard, those who drowned in failed expeditions, forgotten would-be conquerors, pilgrims and pioneers, whalers, sailors, pirates.

And growing in the black soil, thriving on the constant fertilization by human remains, is every manner of vegetation: taro and pineapple and pumpkin and corn and saffron and cocoa and tea, lush and wild as mud boils in a hot spring.

Suppose the explorer's ships are wrecked along seven treacherous rocks in a gulf, a body of water he dubs The Sorrows, where he establishes a village which grows into a fortress which assimilates, eventually, into the American empire. Suppose, in letters, the explorer claims to have discovered the island he sought after all. Arguably, his star-shaped fortress comes to hold many of the world's wonders within, especially beautiful gardens and orchards, and in the ground beneath it and in the sand all around it, just the same, lay the bones of the less fortunate.

Assuming the above statements are true, which of the conclusions follow logically for why the explorer claims to believe in his own folly?

_ It will increase profits.

_ It will encourage everyone to work harder.

_ It will support the spread of common values.

NOTE: You have completed the second section (Quantitative Reasoning), and may proceed to the third section (Qualitative Reasoning).

Q: When you consider your earliest memories, whose love ensures survival and whose attention is a force to be dodged?

_ Childhood is a void to be approached and circled but never ventured into.

_ Recovered memories come back emptier and more fragmented than when you started.

_ None of the above. Childhood is a myth invented by the Victorians.

Q: When you consider that the responses and habits of trauma can be passed down for generations without conscious knowledge of their origins, whose fear is it when your throat shuts and your joints lock?

_ Cold sweat (a plague permitted to ravage, for you are undesirable).

_ Night terrors (a destructive dynamic that goes

excused and normalized).

_ Black out (taken by force, taken by night, suppressed by law, by drink, by your own hand).

_ White out (a language and a custom eradicated softly by means of conversion, re-education, love and marriage and sex and family where blending means blending away your distinguishing features).

Q: Who by fire and who by flood?

_ Learning to burn.

_ Learning to drown.

Q: Whose words do you hear long after they are spoken? Whose opinion of yourself do you hold to be true? Whose fault is it this time? Who is going to pick up the tab? Who is going to fix this? Whose walls protect them and whose walls confine? Who has the luxury to worry about the future? Whose homeland and whose frontier? Whose natural resource and whose unmarked grave? Whose memory of a motherland and whose mother? Whose extermination, whose relocation, and whose assimilation is written on your body but redacted from the records? Who wanders and who is lost? Who is willing to accept pain and who is unwilling to acknowledge their comforts because of their pain?

_ Ask God for delusions.

_ Give up.

_ Review what is at stake.

_ Face your light.

_ Look toward tomorrow and its shortcomings.

Q: If you take tomorrow as a true statement, which of the conclusions follow logically?

_ There is no such thing as the end of the world but this also implies that there is no such thing as saving the world, either.

_ There are no open spaces in North America, only opened spaces.

_ All times are troubled times, troubled differently.

_ Delusion is the true nature of evil.

_ Hope is a delusion. It will encourage everyone to work harder.

_ Despair is a delusion. It will increase profits.

_ Not by faith alone are we saved but through Good Works on Earth.

_ Not by faith alone are we saved by through Good Works in outer space.

_ Aliens might be more likely to find you if you are in space already and some of them could be good looking.

_ Slap yourself across the face where your mom can't reach to do it anymore and cut this out, drama queen.

_ Focus!

_ God's light might also be found staying in bed and having a robust panic attack.

   _ Jesus H. Christ himself is not administering this assessment.

   _ When the moon is out, clap for it. Tell everyone to applaud. Shout, "ladies and maties, tonight's entertainment!" Tell everyone that's where you're going. It will support the spread of common values.

NOTE: You have completed the third section (Qualitative Reasoning), and may proceed to the fourth and final section (Behavior and Preferences).

Look at the shape of your city's outermost walls. Trace the fortified star. Star like a distant sun, like a compass rose, like the Queen of Heaven, like the fruit of salvation missing from her outstretched hand, the apple sliced lengthwise revealing five seeds arranged in five points. Look at her tin crown of seven stars with five points each, atop her painted head, above her painted feet, pressed onto the silver face of a crescent moon.

Look at the fog rolling off the Gulf of Seven Sorrows, at the low tide and the clam-diggers out among the seagulls and the scavenging hawks despite the large red signs warning of heavy metal and septic back-flow. Look at the woman on the beach who is weeping in ecstasy. Look at the men trawling the thin sand with their metal detectors and their territorial dogs. Look along the horizon where the seven jagged islets of the Gulf are presently visible, each the mother of a legendary shipwreck from the earliest settler-colonial voyage to the twilight of the shipping industry.

Look at the cold-cold moon over the burning Earth. Look at the rockets that go to the cold-cold moon from the burning Earth. Visualize yourself strapped into a window seat. Accept the chances of critical malfunction and fatal catastrophe in any form of travel but most of all the kind beyond the atmosphere. Decide that you will definitely, absolutely die and make a sign of the cross that turns into a shrug halfway through.

Look for trouble and find it. Go out with your friends. Look at the decor in the bar, and the adornments that set each of you apart. Look at the carefully-designed glitch and look carefully at your instant delight in it and your desire to protect it as though it were your own aberrant personality. Look at the reification of deviance, at the acceptable levels of non-compliance and resistance. Look at the word "revolution" in every advertisement for soft drinks and sneakers, at "compassion" contained in a forty-five-minute weeknight yoga class with the pretense of spiritual practice. Look at these promises accumulate onto your body and then be ritually shed from it. Look at the world outside your body, and remain the same, regardless.

Look at your mother's limp and your city's plans for redevelopment. Look at the places along her kneecaps and her spine where the revolution failed. Look at the places along the side of the road where compassion has died on a night with record freezing temperatures.

Look at the last picture you took of yourself: defiant, "reclaiming" your beauty and your presence against the advertisements for soft drinks and sneakers that would have you feel ugly, against the weeknight yoga class that would have you remain absent. Look at the filter that produces an algorithmic light leak and the suggestion of grease on the lens. Look at how it has lightened your skin and widened your eyes and narrowed your nose. Look at how it memorizes and recognizes you and how well it looks out for you by knowing where you have been and where you are going. God has granted you free will but the police tell you otherwise. They think you have been loitering too long outside the bodega, so you buy a juice barrel with your bus money and walk home. It's almost sunrise when you return. Your feet are blistered over and bleeding with free will. Your mother may not ask where you've been all night but she already knows. There are eyes on the back of her head.

Look how fondly you take to your childhood bed even though your childhood was anxious and unhappy. Look at how your friends believe they have discovered despair and invented withdrawal and try to identify where the textures of indifference in your lives are the fingerprints of nature, or God, or society. Look at yourself in the mirror constantly or not for weeks on end. It is possible to be conscious of the myriad overlapping systems of oppression that are against you and still be wrong. It is possible for one's anger to be justified and one still to be a jerk. It is possible to learn the less humane lessons from so-called practicality, to fall in love with your own sadness even as you long for relief. Look how nostalgia appears to gives meaning to this tragedy, gives purpose even to despondency. Look for salvation in personal liberation and a revolution of the spirit. The cyberpunks lost, and all that remains is nostalgia, which is an acid that eats meaning.

Your deity rolls back her eyes in every icon and statuary. Look at her from the periphery of your faith so that she can see you in return. Do you love her, or, are you so desperate for recognition you will seek it even when it destroys you? Stand behind your mother when you decide to leave her, and look into the eyes on the back of her head. Tell her where you're going and break her heart. Look to the stars. Look at how the winners get history and the losers get culture. Close your eyes and ask God for light and look for it.

Press save. Press submit. Press submit again to confirm. Submit as in send, submit as in surrender. Confirm as in verify, confirm as in initiate.

Hello?

Are you there?

Are you still there?

Are you still with me?

Can you hear me now?

Come back, Sebastian. You are shaking. That is not a productive movement. It's time to hold still again, to quiet our body and give it over wholly to the future.

VII.

The bus from Stella Maris Central Terminal to the launch site leaves twice daily. Sebastian could take a series of different other private bus lines there from his neighborhood and arrive either three hours early or twenty minutes late for either, which is just so perfectly useless it makes an excellent excuse for him to ask Yonatan for a ride.

"I can't believe my personality was assessed as acceptable?" Sebastian says. With his left hand, he's sipping the goopy remains of a frappe from a drive through shake-n-steak place, and with his right hand, he is holding his phone. He swipes between home screens and different apps in a purposeless loop (the Daily Examen one, a digital tarot card-of-the-day, the 1,492 unread messages in his email inbox).

"I can," Yonatan replies. "They'll take anymore. I mean, but also you're, like, good. Space is the place."

They pass the original Central Terminal on their way, about a mile closer to the center of town than where they're headed. The old train station sits dark, and has for as long as Sebastian can remember. The precious stone and metal inlay of the facade are long scavenged, and he's only seen the stained glass in the tall, boarded windows in old photographs. On a brick by brick basis, little of the old public structures of Stella Maris remain intact except its walls.

"I'll come back eventually, if I don't die," Sebastian says.

"Yeah, you better. Come back, I mean." Yonatan is distracted by a treacherous left turn at an intersection, but fills the silence with fake-real reassurance. "Have fun. Make good choices. Use a moon condom and don't take moon drugs unless they seem really, really fun."

"Don't worry about me," Sebastian plays along. "I'm so holy already, I don't even need a vow of chastity or poverty or any of it. I'm already on it, broke as a joke and haven't swiped my vee-card." Sebastian draws out the vee sound. "Utterly without sin over here," Sebastian continues. "Or serotonin, or job skills. A complete package, really."

Yonatan finally makes the turn, and pulls the car up to the curb of the bus stop, a low fiberglass awning over a single steel bench about a hundred yards from the western-most city gate. The car doors are unlocked and the front windows half rolled down.

"So, uh," Yonatan unbuckles and turns to face Sebastian, who is already as twisted towards Yonatan as he can be in the bucket seat.

Yonatan holds Sebastian's gaze and leans forward. There is a slight receptive parting to his lips, which are exquisitely taupe and round, Sebastian thinks, like one of those Renaissance paintings that make holding a basket of fruit look slutty.

Sebastian flares with the mysterious inside-itch thing. It is getting worse and spreading out. He doesn't know how exactly he is going to scratch it but it also might not matter because if they are about to kiss—oh God; he hadn't brushed his teeth; but also, oh God—then he is about to hecking die and meet Jesus anyway.

"So, um." Sebastian stalls without a plan. "So." He leans forward and kisses the crown of Yonatan's head, waits for the world to crash to an end because of it, and when it doesn't, he moves to Yonatan's lips.

But there, he is less well received. Yonatan and his apoco-lips turn gently aside, and Yonatan lets the kiss land on his soft cheek instead.

Sebastian bursts into flames, he is pretty sure, but can not discern if the burning is pleasure or pain. Or maybe the heat and the car exhaust and the caffeine in the frappe are so strong that the vapors were sending him into anaphylaxis. Or maybe this is Grace? Right? How is he supposed to tell the difference between Grace, infatuation, and allergies?

"Sorry," Sebastian says. "I just. Sorry."

"It's okay," Yonatan says. "I know you like me. Like, have a crush on me. Yeah?"

Sebastian's voice cracks up and snaps out the word, "Yeah," with all the music of a belch through a kazoo.

"And I know, you know, we're both relatively young," Yonatan continues. "But, I'm still a few years older than you."

"Not that many!" Sebastian offers.

"It is, though." Yonatan thinks for another moment. "It's even more when we're young, I think." He says it kindly, like the years between them are not an uncrossable barrier, but a wondrous expanse ahead. "Besides," he adds, "I am looking for a husband, not a boyfriend, and it's not because of your body—that's not an issue for me, pinky promise, plenty of cis men can be good looking—it's just even if you *were* older, you're still, uh—"

"A goy."

"That's a word for it, yeah. I was going to say—"

"I'll convert," Sebastian interrupts. "That's a thing, right?"

Yonatan laughs, but what is the joke? Is it them? Maybe everything in the universe is so connected and interdependent that Grace is also infatuation which is also allergies which is also the past, present, and future.

Yonatan plucks at Sebastian's jacket. Pinback and enamel buttons of Sergius and Bacchus surround an iron-on patch that reads PROBLEMATIC FAVES in Comic Sans.

"You'd have to give these up," Yonatan says. Then he nods and glances askew at Sebastian's lock screen. "You'd have to do it sincerely. Her too."

The background on Sebastian's phone is a picture of *Virgin on a Crescent Moon* (Medieval, Gothic; Materials: wood and polychrony; Collections: Marine, Age of Divinely-Inspired Discovery, Early America, Colonial Stella Maris, Significant Works; "While her approximate age can be verified, her provenance is one of the greatest controversies among Marian scholars today, though she is a favorite of the faithful and secular alike. She is widely believed [1] to have made her passage across the Atlantic Ocean as the figurehead of a galleon in the fleet of explorer and city-founder Iacomo di Santa Sede [2]. Evidence suggests that her outstretched arm originally held a second, smaller sculpture in a different material [3]. Thought many assume this missing piece to be a figure of the Christ Child, descriptions of Iacomo di Sante Sede's ships mention only Mary and never Jesus [4]. Some historians argue [5] that she grasped a gilded apple or pear, the golden fruit of salvation. She is extremely vivid and appealing to the viewer. Wearing a crown of stars and standing upon the crescent moon with a face below, this warm and lyrical image also associates the Virgin with the biblical Woman of the Apocalypse.").

"Hm, so." Sebastian wonders aloud. "How big would someone have to be to stand on the moon like it were a basketball?"

"Well, probably four million feet, give or take. I don't know. Large. *Suspiciously* large for 'someone' who is 'merely venerated' and not worshiped as a goddess."

"Mm... You know, I would sincerely give up all the other saints for you, I think. But it's probably impossible for me to get rid of her. I just mean, if she's that's that big, where else am I going to put her?"

"Seb..."

"I'm really, really, really, really sorry."

"It's really, really, really, really okay," Yonatan says. "I'm sorry, too." Yonatan leans into Sebastian's long arms, allows himself a deep breath, closes his eyes.

In the air is the cool, dry exhale of asphalt at night, and a breeze off the Gulf by way of the Spirit District: salt, sage, gasoline, pork, flowers, frankincense, beeswax. All things burning, brewing, and frying. Sebastian's blood comes to a boil, he's pretty sure. His nerves flash like a fire alarm.

More people arrive and wait for the same bus. Everyone looks straight out of luck. Defunct service cyborgs, addicts, migrants, drop-outs, single parents, estranged children. In dozens of eyes and ocular sensors are hundreds of visions of their shared future. The moon promises them all so much; its surface and its light steady where fortunes and divinations and prayers alone can not suffice; they are moving, instead, into the next phase of their lives, hundreds-of-thousands of miles apart from the institutions that have failed them.

The bus pulls in late and everyone stirs and gathers their belongings. Sebastian has only his backpack stuffed with clothes and headphones and snacks, and his clarinet in its case. He says goodbye to Yonatan, who makes him promise to text when he arrives, if possible.

In line, a security guard briefly questions Sebastian about what his clarinet does, and seems skeptical when Sebastian shows him, but eventually Sebastian is permitted to board the bus. It departs. It passes through the gate. Sebastian tries to memorizes everything he sees as it rushes past. He has only a partial view from the aisle seat, and what little remains blurs through tears.

The bus passes through a shantytown, and then it crosses a desert that used to be called something else. Sebastian tries to remember what. Even language betrays him eventually.

A sunburn? A superb? A suburb.

One year, he isn't sure if it was last year or the year before, at the start of Lent, a priest at Stella Maris Cathedral took ashes in his hands and drew a cross with his finger on Sebastian's forehead, and the priest, smiling, told Sebastian, "You are a child of God, and you come from ashes, and to ashes you shall return," and Sebastian forgot to say "Amen" or be solemn or a normal level of joyful, so he scrambled the script with something else—it must have been, an old black-and-white family movie—and shouted at the priest, "Gee, thanks, mister!"

The buildings are leveled to concrete foundations. Some retain their front steps and walkways, ascending to nothing. One still has a mailbox, overtaken by hornets.

Later there are scrap yards, brimming and sorted.

One pile just of hot tubs. A lot of very specific things like that, hard to re-purpose things. No cars, no computers, no fridges and ovens. Nothing Lara can pocket. No tableau of excess and its follies. Just the arresting sight of hundreds of brightly striped stunt canons, like the kind circus clowns shoot out of.

A cinnamon dune of rust beneath the last grizzle of some gigantic iron building. Half-buried bones of a metal Leviathan. A green pond which bubbles and exhales a yellow fog.

Wild hops and tomatoes in the cracks between the tar and the asphalt. Feral creatures, some of them animals. What remains of the vermin and the scavengers and the small things that gather what is left behind, and make a life from it.

The bus approaches the launch facility, its suites, outbuildings. A representative from _____, wearing a crisp uniform, wearing a pleated smile, carrying a rigid clipboard, rises from the front row of the bus seats and hands out branded pens and contracts still warm and sour from the copy machine.

The terms and conditions. Lump sum payment in bold with yellow highlight. Fine print: no benefits, at will, no liability, health and safety waiver, responsible for own expenses, responsible for own taxes, no holidays, no visits back until the termination of the contract. Everyone on the moon is essential personnel.

A sub-clause in the health and safety waiver. Oblique reference to the high correlation between space travel and cancer, joint pain, vision loss.

Sebastian's eyes, good enough for now, wandering back to the payment figure as intended. It's more money than he'll ever see by any other kind of work he could get, money that doesn't really exist for people like him since they abolished the minimum wage.

A conditional return "ticket" is stapled to the contract like a credit card offer, premature and tantalizing. All marketing.

Sebastian might like to change his mind by going back in time to never having made a decision at all. Linear time is so confrontational. He cannot stand it. He's sweating. He digs through his backpack for his medications in their thin plastic tubes. He spins a container over in his palm, and the cylinder turns and turns with a rattle like soft rain on a Sunday morning. If he takes enough of them, if he takes all of them at once, at least he won't mind when a machine part critically fails—he is sure it will—during launch, when he breaks apart in the atmosphere, when he dissolves in unimaginable heat and radiation. He's only so much water vapor and bad skin held together by atmospheric pressure, after all.

There is a hexagonal tarmac. Pipes and wires. A shuttered dome. Operations, offices. Long shadows of the rising sun. The moon, the moon, the moon.

There is signing the contract and handing it off.

Inspection. Boarding. Harness.

A smell like when things are new but have been in storage for a long time before they're opened.

Dozens of eyes and ocular sensors.

Pre-launch checklist.

Launch checklist.

Countdown.

Ignition.

Sebastian imagines his mother at this moment. He pictures her praying to Saint Christopher under her breath as she waits at the gate outside one of the private communities where she cleans. He imagines that she might feel shy about him imagining her this way, demure that she is merely "Catholic with a small-c," or that it is merely the way she was raised, as though the ways in which one is brought up are of trivial consequence. He can almost hear her explain it just the same, and through a sigh admit that she is running out of options, wonder: was prayer the same as turning away from your problems? Or was it a part of facing them? She didn't know and didn't want to know, not anymore.

She might whisper, all while doubting, "Please protect my son, please if you can, protect Sebastian on his full bodily ascent into the heavens," thinking: it was worth a shot.

And then the gate buzzes and Sebastian's mother pushes herself within, dragging her arsenal of buckets and rags and solvents across a front garden of white polished stone and Japanese maples. A near-silent drone glides hypnotically among the stones, raking them into perpetual order: spirals and circles, waves as gentle as light, almost too long to see. Ambient loops of synthetic birdsong and standing bells play through discreet speakers mounted in the trees. What does Sebastian's mother think of this new fashion for the high-end residences? Does she find it relaxing, inspiring, boring, threatening? Does she think about the Age of Sail and the ceramics and silks and furniture made for export to the West that arrived on tall ships in the first gilded age of the city? Does she recognize the present using this past, the decorative mystification, the fiber-optic Occidentalism?

At the interior guardhouse, Sebastian's mother signs into a guest book and waits for her client to approve her final entry to the building. The guard informs her that the client wishes to come down and greet her personally, and Sebastian's mother maintains her composure though she shoots the guard a side-long glance when he turns back to his computer.

Perhaps it used to be that people who hired "help" didn't want to see or hear Sebastian's mother, and now they want to pretend to be friends with her, flip the transaction into transcendence. Energy frequencies and empathy and setting intentions. Health and wellness. Wealth and hellness. Sebastian imagines this client stepping off the elevator and tidying a designer scarf around her throat, a throat that is as long and white as a crane's, or a swan's, or some other graceful water bird that he knows better than to approach because they are predators, and viciously territorial, and will hiss and charge and gladly bite your fingers off if you get too close.

Sebastian imagines this avian-looking rich lady greeting his mother and leading her back to the elevator, staring and smiling the whole ascent to the penthouse. The rich lady never refers to his mother as a "maid," always a "cleaning person." The rich lady could easily purchase a fleet of custodi-droids but finds such robots sort of sad, calls them something like, "another step on the path away from nature." The rich lady tells her friends that her marriage with her also-rich husband is egalitarian because, with Sebastian's mother, the rich couple need never argue about chores or worry over the gendered division of domestic labor. The rich lady and her husband both wear rare gemstones on their wedding bands, for equality.

The rich lady loves that Sebastian's mother has a stout body and deepening lines in her face, and therefore—the rich lady imagines— she poses no sexual threat, either, but the rich lady keeps this last thought private to herself.

"How are you, Donna?" The rich lady might ask, believing that knowing his mother's name gives her the right to use it.

And, "Oldest still hasn't settled down," his mother says, and, "Middle still traveling," and, "Youngest finally has a job."

And the lady replies, "I asked, how are *you*? How is *your* life?"

And his mother thinks: the nerve of this woman. And says, "My children *are* my life."

And the lady's smile tenses. "Oh," she says. "Of course."

And they spend the remainder of the ride to the sixtieth story in silence.

Sebastian imagines that his mother starts working in the rich people's massive kitchen and works her way through the guest and master bathrooms, even checking the pH balance of the salt-water toilets, and that when she comes to the living room beside the rooftop patio and a statue garden, she stops before the full-length windows. From this height, the other skyscrapers look like great manicured fingers pointing out of hell, and Sebastian's mother can see far past the walls of the city, over the haze of the outlands, all the way to an encasement of mountains, jagged and exhumed of their ore. And his mother sees him, there in that location called the middle distance, the distance that novels are always talking about, beyond the walls and before the mountains: the gray flume and blue torchlight of the rocket carrying Sebastian and all of his new colleagues to the lab-base-dorm-station waiting for them all to run on the moon. From this city, this godforsaken city, from their stations in its societies, there is no way around and no way through. The only way out is up.

And the rich lady sees Sebastian's mother staring into the day and mistakes it for distraction by the glare. The rich lady speaks to the blinds and they close in on the view, and Sebastain's mother turns on her client. She is thinking, this woman wants to pretend that they are peers? She can have it.

"Open them back up," his mother barks, and the lady almost trips on the force of the words.

"Excuse me?" She stammers.

"The blinds, ma'am. Open them again."

And the lady says, "Donna—" and tries to ask what about, but Sebastian imagines that his mother does not wait to respond. She marches up to the glass and places her gloved hands against the image of the shuttle, shrinking away to space between her thumbs, rising, rising, rising, without incident, into a darkness beyond. People in novels are always drifting or marching or gazing into unknowable darknesses, futures, desires, consequences; Sebastian's darkness is well known; his future is pre-written; his desires are their own consequences.

Sebastian understands now how his family are more alike than different. Each, in their own way, loves what hurts them. At first you love what hurts you because you don't know anything else is possible, as though it were intuitive to hold a knife by the blade. You do this long enough and your wounds may not heal but they do grow familiar. You do this your whole life, and the handle becomes a weapon in its own right, the blood-letting extension of your grasp. Now you are no longer so helpless. Now you are a calloused palm wielding a bludgeon, and that's not nothing. You cannot cut, but you can strike. You cannot sever, but you can crush. That can be the way you reach out and touch whatever it is that you need from the world. That can get the job done.

Sebastian imagines that his mother unlatches the French doors of the penthouse and steps out onto the rooftop, out onto the balcony. The marble statues in the garden, the pale stone patio, all those opaline peaks and craters surround her like an earthly mirror to the lunar surface.

"That's my youngest going up there," his mother says. Her eyes well with tears. Pride, anxiety, everything floods forward. And the rich lady is not bothered by this, indeed she is downright satisfied at last, finally able to drink in the pathos of his mother's genuine emotional expressions.

"That's my baby. That's my son in the ship. In the ship."

Sebastian's mother repeats it again and again. And the moon seems enormous to her, as though Sebastian is not moving away towards it at all, but instead it is moving towards the Earth, just for him. "That's my baby."

Again and again and again. Sebastian can almost hear her saying it. And there is no need for him to review the day or look forward to tomorrow and the days to come. And there is no need to ask God: the light is here.

FIRST CONTACT, COMMUNION

Before you left for Mars, you asked me a question.
Now that you're there, I have so many of my own.

Are you meditating atop Olympus?
Do you pray for signs of life?

The way I grew up, everyone kneels and receives
a wafer and a sip of grape juice. I thought
it was the things outside me that were holy,
only briefly tasted. I mistook communion
for a pledge of penitence to everything I could not know.

Do you find solace inside a dust storm?
Can you hear red sand lashing against your body,
just above a whisper?

In the canyons, did you encounter my yawning awe
as I observed the red starpoint of your planet
rise above a dark jetty, and accepted how
it was the closest we could possibly be?

I don't want to feel better; I want to know better.
I should have known that God is not in the meal
but in the sharing of the meal. I should have told you
that holiness resides in needing each other,
in acts of survival made generous.

Is it your heart, that planet? Do you love me?

I owe you an answer.
I've placed it in the candle of a paper lantern,
not in the flame but in the lighting of the flame,
and I'm releasing it at the end of the jetty,
letting it lift off like your ship,
knowing it won't come back to me.
It flickers to a starpoint against the darkness
until it perfectly eclipses my view of your rising red body,
until it arrives there as if by grace alone.

I AM A BEAUTIFUL BUG!

For many years, I longed to be an enormous insect. One day, I learned there was a plastic surgeon in Mississauga, Ontario famous for full-body reconstructive work, and that the exchange rate for my American dollars had never been better! So I booked my appointment, scheduled all two weeks of my earned time off from Super Dollar Gourmet Food Market, and traveled up to see the surgeon. For my convenience, the clinic gave me all kinds of interesting paperwork to do during the long bus trip, and I passed the ride reading and signing releases and disclaimers that I gave my informed consent and accepted full responsibility for satisfaction with my results. I only wish they had given me such a relaxing activity for the return trip, when I needed one even more!

Once at the clinic, I brought my copy of *The Metamorphosis* by Franz Kafka to my brief pre-surgery consultation. I pointed to the inside cover illustration, and said, "Gimme the works, doctor! Just like Gregor Samsa!"

Without blinking, the plastic surgeon said, "Sure can do." He took out a box of neon, rubbery Creepy Crawlers toys and asked me to decide which of their features I wanted to accentuate.

"Oh, a little bit of everything," I said. "I'd like about six legs and the antenna to be as long as you can make them." I picked up a particular bright and colorful Creepy Crawler. "Some fun stripes or dots on my shell, too, if you can?"

He nodded, had me change into paper underpants, and drew dashes, lines, and arrows all over my body with a purple magic marker. Then his assistant set me up with an IV of sedatives and wheeled me into the operating room for the procedure.

When I woke up from my operation, it was exactly like when Gregor Samsa wakes up at the beginning of *The Metamorphosis*, except instead of anxious dreams, I was just nauseous from general anesthesia. I threw up a little, and instead of pink acid from my old stomach, the vomit came up sweet and sticky from a new, secondary stomach! I took a deep breath, and instead of inflating my lungs with air, gases pumped through spiracles along my abdomen and flexed my pneumatic joints! The surgeon had really given me the deluxe treatment.

Excited as I was to get back out there into the big, wide world as a huge, beautiful bug, I had a lot of healing to do first. My mandibles were tender. My antenna ached. My exoskeleton itched something fierce and my half dozen sticky little legs wriggled beneath my surgical dressings in a futile effort to scratch. Also, while I was mostly very large in size, sometimes I shrunk down very small for a few minutes at a time, and then back, which made me dizzy at first.

The plastic surgeon was already working on his next patient, but his assistant told me these were all wonderful signs of recovery or nothing to worry about. Itching and tenderness meant I had circulation and sensation in the tissues, and the grafts and transplants were cooperating with my immune system! The spontaneous changes in size were an unexpected side effect, but the assistant told me just to keep an eye on it and get lots of rest.

The clinic was on the first floor of a shopping mall that sprawled along Hurontario Street. Conveniently, my hotel occupied some of the upper floors of the same mall, so the surgeon's assistant only had to push me on my gurney a short way indoors to help me to my room. I had her unscrew a jar of chitin gel and place it on the nightstand before she left.

In my room, I slept and drank plenty of water. It was easier to drink than I thought it would be, because I could sip the moisture from almost anything. When I felt alert, I gently raised my little wings up and down, back and around, so they didn't get too stiff. I remained mindful and present through several changes in size, and soon found I was able to shrink down oh-so-tiny and back again on purpose! I became small and gingerly crawled into the open jar of chitin gel, burrowing and soaking the slime into my hardening body plates.

My window looked down into one of the mall's food courts. All the shoppers droned and swarmed in their movements below. The sight of them soothed me in my fragile instar state. Despite our differences, it is nice to remember sometimes how we are all really part of the same hive. Unfortunately, not everyone shares this perspective, and when I was cleared to go home at last and made my way towards the bus station in Toronto, I was detained by the United States Border Patrol.

The United States Border Patrol held and questioned me for a very long time. They wanted to know why I seemed so anxious. I told them the truth, which was that if the bus continued without me, I would have to pay for a whole new ticket. This made them decide to hold me even longer. The bus continued without me.

They took away my passport and asked me who I had stolen it from and who I thought I was trying to fool. I showed them all of my other picture IDs, such as my Massachusetts driver's license and my Bank of Benthic debit card, and offered to substantiate my identity further. The one in charge ordered the others to search and frisk me. They put on gloves and prodded about between my segments. They shined bright flashlights into my compound eyes. They even probed my oviduct!

It took them several days to release me, during which I glimpsed that I was only one among many others detained. There were all kinds of people raising the suspicions of the American law enforcement, with diverse traits such as having skin and also names, but certainly I was not the only arthropod, either. They combed through my social media and called several of my contacts. My store manager was asked to fax through proof of my work history and authorization.

"Is this because I'm an enormous insect?" I asked.

"Now ma'am, or sir, we're going to have to ask you to calm down," they said. Their suspicions raised higher and higher, though they would not address the matter of my appearance directly.

My human resources file came through from Super Dollar Gourmet Food Market. Out of respect for the Canadian government, they allowed me to buy a new ticket for the next bus to Boston, but they did not return my passport, licence, or debit card.

The bus pulled into South Station fourteen hours after its scheduled arrival time. It was dark and hazy and the street lights clicked off just as the bus slowed into the berth. I was scheduled to go back to work that very morning, but both the bank and the Registry of Motor Vehicles were on the same block as the bus station, and it would be a real chore to get by without my IDs only to come all the way back downtown another time. I called into work sick.

The bank opened first. I explained my situation to a teller, who directed me to the branch manager. Behind her polished desk, her office window was open. The haze of early morning cleared into a dry, warm, perfect spring day.

She shook her head. "I'm sorry, but we can't update your account information or send you a new card until you can provide a government-issued photo ID reflecting the change. Do you have your passport or licence?"

"No, they were confiscated," I admitted. Her forehead furrowed. "By mistake!" I added. "It's more like they were lost! I'm trying to prevent any further confusion."

The branch manager leaned forward in her leather chair and drew her thin lips into a lemon-sucking frown. "Legally speaking," she said. "I'm afraid we'll have to freeze your accounts for the time being, now that you've reported this."

"Don't you want the most accurate information about me?"

"We cannot accept the risk, unfortunately. You could be attempting to commit fraud or evade creditors. Though we'll be happy to unfreeze your accounts once you have an up-to-date government-issued photo ID."

"I understand," I said, and crawled onto her desk. She shrieked as I darted across the shiny surface and dove out the window, tearing a lovely hole in the screen. My hindwings were still numb, and my forewings still a little twitchy, but they worked! I flew all the way around the corner to the Registry of Motor Vehicles.

The line was long, but if I queued into it right away and stayed awake standing in it through the night, I might have my turn inside as soon as the following morning! I called work again to inform them that I was going to be sick tomorrow, too.

The store manager, the one who had faxed my work history to the United States Border Patrol, answered the office phone and drew a long, audible breath at the sound of my voice.

"I'm worried about your focus and commitment to Super Dollar Gourmet Food Market," he said.

"I'm healing much slower than I thought," I said, and forced a weak trill as much like a cough as I could manage.

"Mm. Look," he said. "If you fail to clock full time hours this many weeks in a row, including your time off, we have to drop you down to part time without benefits, like, disability leave and health insurance, for example."

"What should I do if I stay sick for a while?"

"You'll have to have it approved ahead of time."

"Well, you can count on me!" I said. Car horns, shouting pedestrians, and sirens zoomed past me as I scuttled along the sidewalk outside the Registry of Motor Vehicles. "I'm heading back from the doctor's right now, and I think I'm already feeling a bit better. It'll be an early dinner of chicken noodle soup and ginger ale for me tonight, then straight to bed!"

"It's nice to hear you choosing the right attitude," the store manager said. The volume of his voice trailed away through the sentence. "See you tomorrow morning." The office phone landed in its cradle with a click like a beetle on its back.

I took on extra shifts for several weeks to make up for my lost time, but the Registry of Motor Vehicles was only open during the same hours as the store, and my paychecks continued to be directly deposited to my frozen accounts.

I asked to receive paper checks instead, but there was an indeterminate wait before the switch would take effect. For those weeks I made as many meals as I could from free samples and returns, and begged, borrowed, and stretched my pocket change. I saved enough sidewalk pennies for a single can of beer from the liquor and specialty section, but of course, when my fellow Super Dollar Gourmet Food Market teammates had to card me at the register, I had no proof of my age.

"Aw, come on," I begged my favorite co-worker. "You know it's me."

"Sorry," they said, possibly the only person to ever apologize to me and mean it. "We'll both just get in trouble."

I worked harder than ever with my stiff and tender new body. Yet, each night between my double shifts, I failed to sleep more than a few restless hours at a time. I paced about my studio apartment on Commonwealth Avenue. I climbed the walls and the ceiling. It was not quite fun, per se, but it was distracting to scuttle across the eggshell paint with my many dirty feet. I saw no further use in showering when filth accumulated on me in such interesting new ways. I made myself small and crawled in and out of cereal boxes and peanut butter jars and then scurried in circles around the kitchenette and through the bathroom, leaving greasy and crumbly trails. Some nights I worked myself into quite the frenzy with the expired foods I took home from work. I marveled at the blooms of bacteria and fungus on the meats, the smoky-blue blossoming over the rinds of the cheeses, the herbal vinegars that bubbled, rose, and floated atop the spoiled smoothies and juices. I was wrung out, filthy, but full.

When the landlord came looking for the rent I couldn't pay, I shrunk as teeny-tiny as possible and hid inside the kitchen sink. He let himself in with his special key, took one step into the apartment, and to my relief, he did not come looking for me any further than that. My many footprints all across the walls and ceiling dazzled and distracted him instead, and he rushed away without a word!

"Phew!" I hissed since I could not quite sigh anymore. Then I expanded until I was big enough to fill the entire apartment, and I thought my hardest about how to show a good attitude and accept full responsibility for my own satisfaction. I decided to be more patient and better consider the feelings of others. So, I waited and waited until the slow weeks at work, until the fateful day I had only a single, evening shift. On that morning, I spent my few remaining coins on the downtown express bus fare, and made it to the Registry of Motor Vehicles. Finally! I filled out their relaxing array of forms as neatly as I could while passing those final, exciting hours in line.

When it was at last my turn, I presented everything to the clerk. "Hello there!" I said to her. "I hope you are having a great day today! Here is my change-of-information form, which as you can see, is complete! I'll need a new photo and a new card today, as you can probably see! Ha-ha!"

"You got the permit?" she asked. "You need the third-party metamorphosis permit with the original signature."

"One must have a permit to update a photo?"

"Uh, yeah, 'one must', smart ass," she said, and she stretched her arms out and appealed to the dozens of shelves stacked high with various files.

"Well," I said. "May I have one?"

"I dunno, may you? I don't hand them out, I process them. You're going to have to apply for one at the Courthouse, pick it up there, have it signed by a licensed entomologist, and come back when you have everything in order."

"Fellow laborer, you must be very tired from such a long day!" I said. "I'm so sorry to have wasted your time." I was terribly embarrassed and rushed from the clerk's counter, up the wall, and onto the ceiling of the waiting room where I thought I might take a moment to shriek without bothering anyone else. Unfortunately, this backfired.

I frightened several people, but I felt so, so bad about it! I should have asked the plastic surgeon to make me invisible as well, if I were really smart and considerate, but I was foolish and selfish instead. The cries and commotion in the waiting room drew the upper managers from their offices. One manager introduced himself as the Director of Diversity and Inclusion.

"I'd like to personally apologize for the negative experience you've had," he said, and swiped at me with the business end of a broom. "If you will come down, I'd like to see what we can do to make it right."

"Let me have my picture taken without a permit?" I chirped.

"Other than that," he said, and took another swipe, but the bottoms of my six feet were powerful suction cups and I would not budge.

"It seems unnecessary to have a third party confirm that I am a large insect when, indeed, it's quite apparent," I said. "It's a tad invasive, speakingly only for myself, but it must be extra paperwork on your side, too. You would not want to have a discrimination lawsuit on your hands."

"We strive to treat everyone with dignity and equality at the Registry of Motor Vehicles," the director said. "Though, you do realize the bug in the Kafka story is a metaphor, right? The author did not want the story illustrated. It's meant to be ambiguous, symbolizing alienation and self-denial. The real metamorphosis of the title is actually the sister's coming of age—"

"I am not a metaphor," I said. "I need my driver's license, and I would like to update my photograph, please."

"I wrote a paper on Kafka in college," the director scoffed. "I think I know what I'm talking about." He climbed up onto a waiting room chair to get a better reach and aim on me with the broom. Just as he lunged it towards my head, I fluttered off the ceiling towards his head, bothered him about the face, and zoomed away over the snaking lines and out the double doors.

My shift started soon, and I had yet to eat breakfast or lunch or change into my smock. I rushed home, but there was someone waiting for me outside my apartment door. An exterminator had come.

"Landlord said something about an infestation?" He asked me.

"Oh, no, actually," I replied as I unlocked the door and hurried inside. "No infestation. I have a lease. I live here."

The exterminator pressed forward before I could close the door and barged in after me. "And the rest of the colony? How many have you seen?"

"It's just me," I said. "Just the one."

"There's never just one," the exterminator grumbled. He set down his kit on my carpet. I could either get ready for work in time or rescue my personal belongings before he finished setting up.

I grabbed some marmalade and escaped just as the clouds of poison billowed from the end of his spray nozzle. Super Dollar Gourmet Food Market would have to do without my focus and commitment once and for all, but I chose in that moment to have a joyful attitude. I chose to be ecstatic, even! I was a huge, beautiful bug! Hooray!

Once outside the building, I smashed the driver's side window of the exterminator's truck, hot-wired it, and made off westbound on the carriage roads of Commonwealth Avenue. I trilled and buzzed and chirped out into the air. I hissed and strummed as hard as I could stridulate my limbs together while maintaining control of the truck.

Very soon, my calls were answered by other insects in the area! Hundreds and then thousands of them darted out from grates and crevices, flew down from on high, and enveloped the truck as we continued through the suburbs. We linked our many legs and formed a great and wondrous bug ball, the truck's weight serving merely as our center of gravity. By the time we hit the Mass Pike in Newton, I didn't even have to drive it anymore!

The exterminator had been totally correct. Of course there was more than one of us! I was impressed by how different and yet equally beautiful we all were. Plus, on average, we were quite venomous, too. Our shirking, shrieking hive progressed ever-onward, first northbound towards one national border and then back around, southbound, towards the other, and grew ever-larger and ever-louder on our merry way. Yipee!

We sawed and bored and chewed across North America! We clogged and encased those who would detain us or others with regurgitated fibers and secreted wax, acid, and oil!

Here and there, just for fun, we lay our eggs in the orifices of our enemies, though I admit my once-probed ovipositor took some personal enjoyment from this (tee-hee-hee). I let my beautiful invertebrate body expand to its maximum capacity and sink to the middle and the bottom of the mass with the other decomposers. Down there together, we rolled up all the land we passed through into a dung ball like no one had ever seen before, turning all of it over and over into something a bit more positive.

THE THING IN US WE FEAR
JUST WANTS OUR LOVE

This disease is a motherfucker. It lies to us in our own voice.
So, please: be careful. We may do each other
as much immeasurable harm as immeasurable good
when we get together—once weekly in a moon-
less annex of the community health center, soon
to be absorbed into the hospital conglomerate metastasizing
its way across these black forests—though we hope
to tame that animal we share, or at least, to muzzle it.

But I think it's less about acceptance of how we change than
the social worker would have us believe, and more about the fear
we carry through the rest of each month, when we don't. See,
I know that we can love the dangerous creature we are at night,
so how do we love the form of the powerless, naked body
it takes by day? How do we howl when the sound is lost?
The monster will take what it wants, that is what makes it
our monster, but how can we tend to the sleeping beast?

NOTES

THE MARKS OF AEGIS was first published in *Third Point Press* in 2017.

HEAR YOU ARE, NEAR ME was first published in *Five:2:One* in 2016.

SELF CARE was first published in *Nat. Brut* in 2019. Thank you to Nisi Shawl for her feedback on an early draft, and to Tony Wei Ling for championing its final form. It is dedicated to Julie Blair, whose whole deal has been a creative influence that can hardly be measured.

THE NOTHING SPOTS WHERE NOBODY WANTS TO STAY was first published in the *Procyon Science Fiction Anthology* in 2016, and has appeared as a reprint in *Transcendent 2: The Year's Best Transgender Speculative Fiction* from Lethe Press in 2017. Thank you to the unstoppable Bogi Takács for eir invaluable editorial and curatorial work in the genre, and for inviting me along for the ride.

THE HEAVY THINGS was first published in *SmokeLong Quarterly* in 2017, and has appeared as a reprint in *Transcendent 3: The Year's Best Transgender Speculative Fiction* from Lethe Press in 2018.

THE SEED AND THE STONE was first published in *The Fairy Tale Review* in 2018.

WE DID NOT KNOW WE WERE GIANTS incorporates paraphrasing and light quotations from the Biblical Book of Job, as well as *John Muir: His Life and Letters and Other Writings* by John Muir.

THE ANDROID THAT DESIGNED ITSELF was first published in *Rosalind's Siblings* from Galli Books in 2019.

AS TENDER FEET OF CRETAN GIRLS DANCED ONCDE AROUND AN ALTAR OF LOVE was first published in *Strange Horizons* in 2017. What scant factual bases do exist for the majority of the archaeological and historical details are adapted from *Knossos and the Prophets of Modernism* by Cathy Gere. The title is a quotation from *Sappho: A New Translation* by Mary Barnard.

ESTRANGED CHILDREN OF STORYBOOK HOUSES was first published in *Hypocrite Reader* in 2018. Thank you to Kit Eginton for pushing me to ask more of myself for it.

MY NOISE WILL KEEP THE RECORD was first published in *Paper Darts* in 2017. According to vague personal recollections on the part of the author, the line about Pavlov is, maybe, a variation on a Tumblr meme that has proven impossible to source despite diligent efforts, because Tumblr was not good.

WAKE WORD was first published in *Reflex Fiction* in 2017.

EVERYONE ON THE MOON IS ESSENTIAL PERSONNEL is dedicated to Tomás Ruiz. Additionally, special thanks is owed to Jeanne Thornton, a brilliant and tireless editor, who believes in and enables misfit stories, and provided crucial insight on this one.

I AM A BEAUTIFUL BUG! was first published in *Maudlin House* in 2019. It is primarily informed by the work of Franz Kafka, in particular *The Castle* and *The Metamorphosis*. It was written in a bad mood, atop in an uncomfortable chair, inside of a poorly ventilated room, while listening to the Katamari Damacy theme song on a ten-hour loop.

THE THING IN US WE FEAR JUST WANTS OUR LOVE was first published in *Uncanny Magazine*, Issue 30: Disabled People Destroy Fantasy in 2019. The title is borrowed from the text of a fortune cookie that the author received and consumed in a depressing corporate cafeteria.

In general, this collection is the result of the encouragement, assistance, and criticism of countless friends, acquaintances, colleagues, readers, editors, enemies, entities, and all the other cool freaks who did it first. Thank you. The material fact of this book would be impossible without the work of Steve Berman, Leah Paulos, Bri Kane, Peter Barnfather, and Kim Hu. More abstractly, but just as crucially, further gratitude is owed to Jeanne Cavelos and the Odyssey Class of 2018 for structure and follow through, Carrow Narby for challenging conversation, Danny Lavery and Casey Plett for generous guidance, Isaac Fellman for deep faith, and Seth Alter for the bravest love imaginable.

ABOUT THE AUTHOR

Julian K. Jarboe is from Massachusetts. This is their first book.

G'nite Fuck-o's
　　— Carrie Fisher

CPSIA information can be obtained
at www.ICGtesting.com
Printed in the USA
LVHW091343080320
649328LV00002B/207

9 781590 216927